A big, high bed. Rumpled, unmade, the sheets tangled around what looked like a duvet.

He closed his eyes with a despairing sigh. It was the rumpled sheets that finished his resolve. The gleaming white tangle of sheets needed to be wrapped around her naked body. And his. And he took the gun from his waistband, set it silently on the dresser by the door, and started toward her.

She must have felt him coming. She turned when he reached her, looking up at him, and there was no fear on her face. He touched her, cupping her cheek with his big hand, and she felt warm, fragile against him.

She turned her face and pressed her mouth against his palm. "You taste of cinnamon," she whispered. And he wanted her to taste him.

She tilted her face up then, brushing her mouth against his, a tentative gesture, as if she weren't sure of her welcome. He slid his arm around her waist, pulling her soft, willowy body against him with careful deliberation, settling her against him, letting her feel how hard he was, and he set his open mouth against hers.

"Don't stop," she whispered, a mere breath of a sound, a plea.

Anne Stuart

MOONRISE

A SIGNET BOOK

SIGNET
Published by the Penguin Group
Penguin Books USA Inc., 375 Hudson Street,
New York, New York 10014, U.S.A.
Penguin Books Ltd, 27 Wrights Lane,
London W8 5TZ, England
Penguin Books Australia Ltd, Ringwood,
Victoria, Australia
Penguin Books Canada Ltd, 10 Alcorn Avenue,
Toronto, Ontario, Canada M4V 3B2
Penguin Books (N.Z.) Ltd, 182–190 Wairau Road,
Auckland 10, New Zealand

Penguin Books Ltd, Registered Offices:
Harmondsworth, Middlesex, England

First published by Signet, an imprint of Dutton Signet,
a division of Penguin Books USA Inc.

First Printing, July, 1996
10 9 8 7 6 5 4 3 2 1

REGISTERED TRADEMARK—MARCA REGISTRADA

Printed in the United States of America

PUBLISHER'S NOTE
This is a work of fiction. Names, characters, places, and incidents
either are the product of the author's imagination or are used ficti-
tiously, and any resemblance to actual persons, living or dead,
events, or locales is entirely coincidental.

This is for Vicki Varvello, who shares
the same twisted taste in movies and men,
and who exemplifies grace under fire.

For Barbara Samuel, a writer
with extraordinary vision, talent and intelligence.

And for Audrey LaFehr, whose wisdom,
good taste and discerning ear are invaluable.

Chapter One

The woman didn't know she had just come closer to death than most people did in their entire lives. She stood outside the door of the ramshackle cottage, her white cotton clothes creased and rumpled from the long trip. In another lifetime that upraised hand that had just knocked on his door would be wearing a spotless white glove, and she'd be wearing a hat on that soft sweep of hair.

He stood in the shadows, watching her. He'd chosen this cottage, this tiny island off the gulf coast of Mexico, for a reason. No one could get anywhere near him without him hearing them from miles away. There was no approach from the rocky beach, and the narrow drive that led through the thick underbrush led nowhere else.

He'd been lying in his hammock, working his way into a bottle of Jose Cuervo, when he'd heard the taxi turn toward his place.

Teo's ancient Buick was unmistakable to a man of his training, no matter how drunk he was. They wouldn't be coming after him in a taxi, he thought as he moved silently, swiftly through the house. He took only one gun with him. One would be enough.

He hadn't recognized her at first. The slender, white-clothed figure climbed out of Teo's taxi, and she carried a case with her. He wondered exactly what kind of weapons she had in that case, and how she'd managed to get them through the surprisingly rigorous customs on the tiny island.

She had to be carrying as well, but as far as he could see there was no room for anything but the smallest gun on that slender body. She could have a knife strapped to her thigh, but she didn't hold herself like someone good with knives, and his instincts, honed over time, were infallible.

The taxi left, and they were alone in the clearing. Night had already fallen—it came early in October, and the moon was beginning to rise, covering the area with a silver light.

In the moonlight, fresh blood would look black.

He stood in the trees, loose, relaxed, alert. He could take her out in a matter of seconds. It was what he was trained to do, what he did best. He could send a bullet into her brain, just behind her ear, judging the distance within a fraction of an inch, and her skull would explode.

Or he could move up behind her, and she wouldn't hear him. Even if her training matched his, she wouldn't be as good as he was. No one was.

And she was too young. Even if she had his talent, she didn't have his years of experience.

He wondered why he hesitated. There was no reason anyone would have come after him, would have gone to the trouble of finding him, unless they were planning to kill him. And he had a cardinal rule—get the bastards before they got you.

They'd tried once, but he thought they'd given up on trying to take him. Obviously not.

He raised the gun. He didn't want to put his hands on her—it had been too long since he'd had a woman, and he wasn't a man who mixed sex with killing. One was a basic need, to be ignored if it grew inconvenient. The other was a job.

She climbed up the sagging front steps, and he noticed she was wearing an incredibly stupid pair of white shoes. High heels. No killer would come after him in high heels.

He slowly lowered the gun and let out his breath. He hadn't realized he'd been holding it. She knocked on the door, and he could read her body language in the silver light. She was nervous. No, beyond that. She was terrified.

So she must know who and what he was. What did she want with him?

Curiosity was a luxury he seldom indulged. There were two choices—to kill her or to send her away.

There was nothing suspicious in the run-down cottage—he'd made sure of that. His cache of weapons was hidden so well the best people in the business wouldn't be able to find them. He could simply fade into the night and wait for her to leave.

He started to back away, tucking the compact Beretta into his belt, feeling the coolness of metal against his hot skin, when she turned her head. And a flash of memory hit him, like a fist in his gut. He knew who she was.

Win Sutherland's daughter. Cherished only child of his mentor, his foster father, the man he'd trusted and loved most in this world. The man who'd given him a new life and a fresh start.

And he hadn't known the price until it was too late.

What the hell was Annie doing there? He hadn't seen her since the funeral, and he'd kept his protective coloring wrapped around him. She'd been so lost in grief she had barely noticed him standing beside her at the grave, but then, he'd always made sure she seldom noticed her father's protégé. He was good at that, at blending in. It was one of the reasons he'd managed to stay alive for so long.

But now she was here. And he didn't know what the hell he was going to do about her.

She'd been a fool to come, Annie thought, rubbing her sweaty palms against the rumpled linen of her skirt. It had taken her more than twelve hours to get here, she was exhausted and hungry and her head ached.

But most of all, she was scared shitless.

She couldn't imagine why she was frightened of someone like James McKinley. She'd known him for most of her life—he'd been a family friend, her father's confidant, a pleasant, polite man who'd pose no threat to anyone.

There'd been a time when he'd seemed more than that. But it was so long ago that it seemed no more than an adolescent dream, one she could barely remember.

McKinley had taken her father's death hard, almost as hard as she had, and no wonder. His death had made no sense. Winston Sutherland wasn't the kind of man to misjudge his capacity for alcohol. He wasn't the kind of man who'd break his neck, tumbling down the back steps of his Georgetown house. And he wasn't the kind of man who'd have his daughter be the one to find his body the next morning, already stiff with rigor. Even in death he would have had too much power over circumstances.

She hadn't been able to wipe that image out of her brain for the past six months. It crept into her nightmares, and nothing she could do would stop it. He wouldn't have had too much to drink. He wouldn't have fallen.

But he had. According to the autopsy, the police, the kind, capable people who'd worked with her father through his various government jobs, it was nothing but a tragic accident. It was a lucky thing he'd left her well cared for. Extremely well cared for. And would she by any chance be interested in selling the house where her father had died and start a new life?

That was when the alarm bells had begun ringing. That was when she started to ask questions, when the first rush of grief and denial had passed. And that's when she first began to recognize the lies.

She had never realized how protected she was. In all her twenty-seven years, she'd never realized just how little she knew about her father's profession. Bureaucrat, he'd called himself, laughing. The job changed with administrations, but in essence he was nothing more than a glorified pencil pusher, he'd assured her. The titles changed, the work remained the same.

But apparently the work hadn't remained. No one filled her father's position in the State Department, and his small sub-bureau no longer seemed to exist. His coworkers, when she finally remembered their names, had been posted to the far corners of the world, including the man who'd been closer to Win than anyone, including his own daughter. James McKinley.

If it hadn't been for Martin, she might never have discovered where he went. James McKinley had been the first, and the closest, of Win's protégés—Annie could never remember a time when McKinley wasn't around. But in the succeeding years her father had had other people, both men and women, who'd come and gone in his life.

Some she'd liked, even loved. Her ex-husband, Martin, was smart, charming, and deferential, everything she could ever want in a man or a lover. She still couldn't figure out why it hadn't worked, when both of them had wanted it to. There'd been other friends, like Alicia Bennett, who'd died several years ago. A surprising number of Winston's protégés had died.

Some she'd despised, like Roger Carew, a smug little toad of a man who always seemed to be sneering at her. Carew had left her father's tutelage, and if Win had been disappointed in him, he'd never said.

And then there was James McKinley. If Martin was more like a brother than a husband, McKinley was an enigma. Distant. Unapproachable. Polite and unreal.

The man who knew the secrets. That's what her father had said years ago. If ever anything happened, anything questionable, she could go to McKinley for the answers, Win had told her in a rare burst of openness.

It had taken her months to remember. But now she was here, having tracked him down with Martin's reluctant help. She was here for answers.

She knocked again. She didn't want to call out his name—she'd never been certain what to call him. Win had called him Jamey, but the nickname had been a joke between the two of them. McKinley had never been a Jamey in his life—he was too austere, too remote.

Martin and Carew usually called him Mack. Annie called him nothing at all.

She banged again. It was dark, and she'd sent the taxi away, afraid that if she'd asked him to wait she might chicken out. "Hello?"

she called out, still avoiding using his name. "Anyone home?"

"Right behind you."

She whirled around, hitting her elbow on the door. She hadn't heard him approach, and in the moonlight she knew an instant's panic as she looked up into the face of a complete stranger.

"What are you doing here, Annie?"

Not a complete stranger after all. She knew that voice, cool and distant, infuriatingly calm. But she didn't know the man who stood far too close to her.

He was McKinley's height, tall, much taller than her respectable five feet eight inches. But there all similarity ended.

She couldn't remember having looked that closely at McKinley when he'd been with her father, not in years. She knew he was tall, ageless, anonymous, dressed in neat dark suits and a calm manner that left her feeling vaguely soothed and irritated at the same time.

This man had nothing to do with that cipher. His hair was long, shaggy, tied back from his unshaven face. His eyes were dark, glittering, and he was wearing cutoffs and a grubby tropical shirt that hung open around his chest. This was no polite cipher. This was an animal, feral, trapped, and very dangerous. He smelled of alcohol.

"Jamey?" she said in disbelief, instinctively using her father's name for him.

He flinched, as if she'd hit him. And then he seemed to straighten, and that sense of danger disappeared. "Your father's the only man who got away with calling me that," he said.

She smiled uncertainly. "Win got away with a lot of stuff," she said.

"Not always. What are you doing here, Annie? And how did you find me?"

"Martin told me where you were."

She could see some of the tension in his shoulders relax. Muscled shoulders. She'd thought he was close to her father's age. She began revising her estimate downward by twenty years.

"Why?" he said again, his voice brusque.

"I want to find out what really happened to my father."

He just stared at her for a moment. "He died, Annie. Remember? He had too much to drink, he fell down the back stairs and broke his damned neck."

"I don't believe it."

"They did an autopsy. I'm sure you can read it if you've got the stomach for it—"

"I saw it. I still don't believe it. Someone's lying. Someone's covering up."

Silence for a moment. "What do you think happened?"

"I think someone killed him," she said, before she could chicken out. "I think he was murdered."

It was growing darker, and faint slivers of moonlight filtered down around them. His face was composed of planes and shadows, and she couldn't see him clearly. Just the glitter in his dark eyes. "What do you expect me to do about it?"

He hadn't denied the possibility, which shocked her. "You were his friend," she said. "Don't you want to know the truth? Don't you want revenge?"

"Not particularly."

She looked up at him, frustration making her grim. "Well, I do. And if you don't want to help me, I'll have to take care of it on my own. I'm going to find out what happened to my father. And I'll be damned if I let them get away with some cover-up."

He didn't move. She had the sudden, eerie feeling that she was in danger. Very great danger. She didn't dare look behind her—if she did, it would be to admit she was scared. So instead she kept her back straight, even though McKinley was close enough that she could smell the alcohol on his breath. She could feel the tension in the air, emanating from his surprisingly strong body.

And then it seemed to dissolve. "All right," he said in a cool voice, putting one hand under her elbow in what should have been a polite gesture. "You might as well come in. We'll talk about it."

She jerked for a moment, then held still. "Does that mean you'll help me?"

"That means," he said in his deep rasp of a voice that held the faintest memory of east Texas, "that you'll tell me everything you know, everything you suspect, and then we'll see what we have to do about it." He pushed open the door, into the shadowy cottage, and she had no choice but to precede him inside. Once more resisting the impulse to look over her shoulder.

She looked around her as he flicked on the electric light. It was a small room, untidy. The furniture was frayed and broken, dishes were piled on the table. She turned to glance at him in the soft light.

"Why are you living here?" she asked. "This doesn't seem like your kind of place at all."

Just the faintest trace of a smile curved his mouth. It was hardly reassuring. "And you know me so well, don't you, Annie?"

"I've known you for most of my life," she said, defensive.

"How old am I?"

She blinked. "You're drunk."

"I didn't ask that. And as a matter of fact," he said, grabbing a chair and straddling it as he poured himself a glass of tequila, "I'm not nearly drunk enough. I've barely made a start on the night's ration." He poured a second glass, pushed it across the table toward her.

"I don't drink."

"You do tonight," he said. "How old am I?"

She took the glass of tequila and allowed herself a faint sip. She hated tequila, and always had. "I used to think you were a little bit younger than my father," she admitted.

"Your father was sixty-three when he died."

"I know that," she said irritably, taking another sip.

"Sit down, Annie, and tell me how old I am."

"Not as old as I thought. Maybe in your late forties."

"Maybe," he said. "So why don't you think your father's death was an accident?"

"Instinct."

"Christ," he said weakly. "A woman's intuition. If that's all you've got to go on, sweetheart, then you're wasting my time."

"My instincts are excellent. Win always said so."

"Yeah," he said, draining his glass. "Well nigh infallible."

"There's something else."

She didn't imagine the sudden tension in the small cottage. "What else?"

"There's something missing from the house. I didn't even realize it was gone until recently, and I know it was there just before he died. I came down from Boston the week before, and it was—"

"What was, Annie? What the hell are you talking about?"

"A picture. He hadn't had it for very long, but he always kept it with him. He said it had sentimental value."

"Your father wasn't a sentimental man. What was it a picture of?"

"Some obscure Irish saint. It never made sense to me, why he should have had it framed in silver, but he said it held the mysteries of the universe."

"Did he?" James drawled. "And you think there's some murderous conspiracy behind an old picture of a saint?"

"It wouldn't have disappeared, not in the week after he died."

"You've been reading too many mysteries, Annie. A tragic accident and a missing piece of religious art do not a conspiracy make." He turned away from her, and his movements had the deliberate grace of a man trying to appear sober.

"When did you become a drunk?" she said sharply. "You never used to be like this."

"April second."

The reply hung between them. It was the day her father had died.

She moved then, skirting the table, coming around to his side and kneeling down in front of him, not even hesitating. "You loved him," she said. "As much as I did. We can't just ignore what happened. Someone killed him, and we have to find out who and why. If you won't help me, I'll do it myself. But you will, won't you?"

He smiled down at her, and perhaps it was meant to be reassuring. Annie wasn't reassured. She didn't know this man—she kept looking for McKinley beneath the stubble and the danger, beyond the tequila and the unexpected look of him. He had to be in there, somewhere.

"Oh, I'll help you, Annie," he said softly. "You'll get the answers to all those questions running about in your head. But I'm not sure you'll like them."

"Liking has nothing to do with it. I'm not going to stop until I find out."

He looked down at her, and there was an odd expression in his eyes. "I know you won't,

Annie," he said gently. "And I'm sorry about that."

He was going to have to do something about her. She knelt at his feet, all sweet-smelling innocence and trust, staring up at him. Her father's age? Christ, he was thirty-nine years old. He'd done his job too damned well.

She was right—he had known her for most of her life. Since she was seven years old and he'd arrived in her life as James McKinley, newly widowed and not long out of college. Ready to follow Winston Sutherland anywhere, do anything he wanted. Ready to expiate the sins that stained his soul. It was a life he'd lived for more than twenty years now. It had become second nature to him.

He knew just how tenacious, how stubborn, how bright Annie Sutherland was. She wouldn't let it go. Not until she learned the unpalatable truth, about all of them. A truth even James didn't know completely.

While Win had been alive he'd been able to shield her. Win had been good at that—he could string together a bunch of lies that could convince the most rabid conspiracy buff that everything was aboveboard. He'd had the advantage with Annie, of course. She'd loved him, trusted him. It wouldn't occur to her to suspect her father of being anything other than the charming, slightly stuffy bureaucrat he'd appeared to be.

But Win wasn't around to cloud her mind anymore. And she'd inherited his brains, even if she'd never used them in the same arena. It would only be a matter of time before she began making some very dangerous enemies.

It wasn't his concern, he reminded himself. He was a dead man already—so what if Annie Sutherland was added to their list of victims?

And he didn't really give a damn if she blew the cover off the whole stinking mess. He'd lost any interest in right or wrong, the good guys or bad guys. He'd spent too much of his life meting out someone else's justice. He no longer cared.

He looked down at Anne. She probably had no idea of the thoughts racing through his brain, that no amount of tequila could deaden. He looked down at her slender, delicate throat, and thought about how much pressure he'd need to exert to break her neck. It would be simple, easy, no more than a flick of the wrist, and she and her questions would be no threat to anyone.

She wasn't a particularly beautiful woman—Winston had seen to that. She wore her brownish blond hair long and simple, her clothes were uninspired, her makeup minimal. She could have been stunning, but Winston was good at manipulating people. He'd wanted a daughter who was moderately attractive, intelligent, and outside the business. A glamorous beauty would have garnered too much attention, so Annie Sutherland's perfect bone structure was hidden beneath a shaggy haircut and a self-deprecating style that was almost as effective as McKinley's protective coloration, even if it wasn't conscious.

He looked down at her, and he wondered what she'd do if he put his hand behind her head and pulled her mouth toward his crotch.

She probably didn't know what to do with that mouth, he thought sourly. Win had scared off any but the most harmless of her lovers. Only his chosen one, Martin, was allowed to get close to her for any length of time. He never knew whether Win had destroyed their marriage in the end, or whether it had simply died a natural death. He told himself he'd never cared.

In the end, James didn't touch her, because he wasn't certain what he'd do. There was no hurry. No one could approach this place without him knowing, and so far they'd done a piss-poor job of coming after him. Annie being there would up the ante, of course, but they'd already let her get this far. Unless Martin had been able to cover it up, but he'd be a fool to count on that.

"Why didn't you ask Martin for help?" he said suddenly. "Or did he turn you down?"

"I wanted you," she said.

The words hung between them. He watched, with drunken amazement, as a faint sheen of color mottled her cheeks. She was actually blushing.

"Annie," he said, suddenly weary, "go to bed."

She glanced around. "Where?"

"There's a bed upstairs. Take it. I've had too much to drink tonight to deal with you. We'll talk about this in the morning."

"Does that mean you're going to help me?"

He rose, caught her arm, and hauled her up. She was slender, the white suit was wrinkled, but she still smelled like some faint, sexy perfume. Not the kind of perfume he would have chosen for her.

"Maybe," he said. "For the time being, get your butt upstairs and out of my sight."

She smiled at him then. Christ, he'd forgotten Annie Sutherland's smile. It had been a long time since he'd seen it, an even longer time since it had been directed at him. It was still just as powerful.

"I knew you wouldn't let me down," she said. She leaned over and hugged him, an exuberant, sexless hug, backing away before he could make a drunken swipe at her.

"I didn't say—"

"I'll see you in the morning," she said, escaping up the narrow stairs. Not knowing how close that escape was.

It was too damned small a house. The upstairs bedroom was nothing more than an open balcony. There was no door on his bedroom either.

He knew, deep in his heart, what he was going to have to do, and all the tequila in the world couldn't change things.

He was either going to have to do his damnedest to convince sharp-eyed, quick-witted Annie Sutherland that her father was a harmless bureaucrat who'd died in a freak accident.

Or he might have to kill her himself.

Chapter Two

Moonlight shone in the office window. It was late, very late, in Langley, Virginia, and the building was relatively quiet.

"We've got a problem, sir."

"Define it."

"It's McKinley, sir."

"That's nothing new. We knew we were going to have to take him out sooner or later. He's holed up in that rathole in Mexico—he's not going any place without our being on him like flies on shit. He's also gonna be damned hard to take if we go in after him. What's the hurry?"

"He's not alone, sir."

"Shit. I should have known. A man with Mack's abilities could sell himself to the highest bidder. People with his talents are always in demand. Who is it? The Iraqis? The IRA? The Red Brigade?"

"Worse, sir. It's Annie Sutherland."

There was a measured pause. "Shit. We'll have to go in, then. We've been playing a waiting game, and time just ran out. You've got the men for the job?"

"I thought I could handle it, sir."

"No way. Mack's more than a match for any single operative I know, and this isn't your area of expertise. You send a team of your best. We can't afford to make mistakes on this one. He's a goddamned killing machine. It's bad enough we've got to lose him. I don't want anyone else going down if we can help it."

"Yes, sir. What about Sutherland's daughter?"

"What about her? You know as well as I do that there's no room for loose ends. For witnesses, for questions. Your people know how to handle these things."

"Yes, sir. When?"

"How long's she been there?"

"My sources said she arrived on the island this afternoon and got to his place by dusk."

"Are you sure he hasn't already solved half our problem? The last man sent in after him wound up dead. He's not the kind of man to wait around and ask questions. Maybe Annie Sutherland's already floating on the tide."

"No, sir. The taxi driver has been in our pay for months. He says McKinley let her in."

"Shit."

"Yes, sir."

"How long will it take you to get a team together? People you can trust? People without sentimental feelings about a coworker?"

"Two or three days. Maybe four at the most."

"I want the job done by tomorrow night. We can't afford to fuck around on this one, son. Your ass and mine depend on getting this right. You know that, don't you?"

"Yes, sir. It'll be taken care of."

"Tomorrow?"

"Tomorrow."

"Good man," said the General, leaning back in his chair. "Let's drink to that."

Annie lay in the narrow bed, sleepless, restless, listening for sounds of movement beneath her second-floor bedroom. She'd been a fool to come, she knew that. But then, she'd been telling herself that, nonstop, for the past three days, since she'd made up her mind to ask James McKinley for help.

It wasn't going to bring her father back. Nothing would, and this stupid quest was probably nothing more than an extreme case of denial. So what if the accident seemed uncharacteristically stupid and unlikely? Most accidents were.

She'd gone through the first stages of

mourning. The anger, the blind denial, the numb grief. It had been more than six months, just about time for her to pull up her socks and get on with her life.

It was a good, rewarding life. She was healthy, young, and reasonably attractive. Even if her short-term marriage hadn't worked out, the divorce had been amicable and civilized, and she and Martin were still friends. Even if her subsequent relationships had never given her exactly what she wanted, they'd been pleasant, mutually satisfying, casual.

She had friends, good friends. She had a job she adored—school psychologist at the same exclusive Quaker school where she'd spent her childhood. She'd moved back to the house in Georgetown, full of memories, of course, but most of them happy ones. And she had enough money for the occasional luxury. More, in fact. She'd never quite realized how much money her father had actually had until she inherited it.

The only thing missing in her comfortable life was love. There was no bringing her father back—maybe she ought to go out and buy a puppy, for God's sake, instead of going on some brainless crusade. Maybe she ought to get married again.

For the past three days coming here had seemed like the logical thing to do. The only thing to do. Go find McKinley. The man who knew the answers.

She'd always thought that absurdly melodramatic of her father. Winston Sutherland hadn't been above a streak of theatrics, of romanticizing things a bit, but that had only made Annie love him more.

Now she wasn't so certain her father had been exaggerating at all. The James McKinley she remembered was a sober businessman, whose only answers would have something to do with government contracts or the like.

But the man she'd seen tonight was a different matter entirely.

She'd half hoped she'd find him sitting in one of his charcoal gray suits, sipping coffee and looking avuncular, and she'd realize how foolish she'd been, to start imagining conspiracies and murder and cover-ups.

But the dangerous creature she'd left in the kitchen of the tiny cottage had set all her alarm bells ringing. She'd meant to broach the subject of Win's death gradually, casually. Instead she'd blurted it out, confronted by a stranger she'd known all her life.

She shouldn't have come, she knew it. As she lay in the bed, sweltering, she knew she had to apologize, and leave, first thing in the morning.

If she had any sense at all.

*   *   *

She didn't know he was watching her. James wasn't the kind of man who made mistakes, and tonight was no exception, despite the amount of tequila he had drunk, despite the shock her appearance had given him.

She lay in the narrow iron bed, her tawny hair spread out around her shoulders. She was wearing some sort of tank top, exposing her long, tanned arms, and the sheet lay tangled around her legs. It had taken her quite awhile to fall asleep, and he'd sat downstairs in absolute silence, drinking his tequila and listening to the sound of her breathing. The very sound of her heartbeat.

And then he'd come up the narrow stairs to stare at her while she slept. If he hadn't been drunk, he wouldn't have touched her hair, moving it away from her tanned neck. The feel it was silky, sliding through his fingers as he exposed her throat. He stared down at her, knowing how very easy it would be to exert just the right amount of pressure. She would die very quickly.

He stepped back, shaken. Damn, he was getting too old for this. He'd had too much to drink, too much to think about. Killing someone wasn't an issue to be debated. It was either orders followed, or instinct.

But he was through listening to orders, and

his instincts, at least as far as Annie Sutherland was concerned, were haywire. He needed to remind himself of the drill. Fall back upon habit if his brain wasn't working right.

He searched her bag soundlessly, methodically. She went in for silk and cotton underwear. Not too plain, not too saucy. Middle of the road, conservative. As Win had molded her.

Her clothes were the same. Classic, conservative, and politically correct. He wondered what politics Win had imbued in her.

There was no sign of a weapon, which didn't surprise him. He'd already come to the conclusion that Annie Sutherland was exactly who and what she appeared to be.

She'd brought her vitamins, enough to stock a health food store. She'd brought tranquilizers and sleeping pills, both prescription. She'd brought a box of condoms. He wondered idly who she was planning to fuck.

He doubted if it was going to be him.

He took her purse and carried it downstairs with him, emptying it out on the cluttered kitchen table. He poured himself another glass of tequila as he sat down to look through it.

Traveler's checks. Ten thousand dollars worth—quite a piece of change for a spur of the moment trip. But then, Win had left her an obscene amount of money. Obscene considering where it had come from. Credit cards, makeup, cash. And a couple of letters.

He recognized the handwriting on both of them. He opened the one from Martin first. Martin Paulsen was the closest thing he had to a friend right now. Which wasn't saying very much. He scanned the letter to Annie, taking in the details with lightning speed, unaffected by the amount of alcohol he'd consumed. She'd slept with Martin, her ex-husband, sometime in the not too distant past. It was over, though perhaps it could be rekindled. And Martin didn't think there was anything suspicious about her father's death. Most of all, he didn't think McKinley would have anything to offer.

Smart man, James thought with a stirring of gratitude. Unfortunately, Annie Sutherland hadn't listened to his good advice. She was here. And they were both going to live to regret it. Though probably not for long, in either of their cases.

He was avoiding the second letter. He knew Win's handwriting as well as he knew his own, and he didn't want to read it. He picked it up, despising his sudden sentimental weakness, and glanced at the date. March 28. Five days before he'd died.

He would have known he was a dead man by then. Exactly what had he told Annie, to make her come after him? Had he guessed the truth, even in advance? Winston Sutherland had been almost supernaturally canny about such things. He probably would have known when and why. Chances were, he would have known who as well.

He smoothed the crumpled letter for a moment. Then he pulled it open and read it.

There was nothing the slightest bit suspicious at first glance. Just fatherly admonitions couched in Win's slightly mocking graciousness. It didn't necessarily sound like a man saying good-bye.

But it was. Win had known he had been found out. His lucrative sideline exposed and his sentence passed down. He'd probably known who would come for him.

James's eyes narrowed. *I'm looking forward to the Irish blessing you're embroidering for me, darling Annie*, the letter said. *When I see it I'll think of you, and I'll think of Jamey. He's a good man. Go to him if you ever need help and I'm not around.*

It was all he could do not to crumple the paper. He folded it carefully, slipping it back into the envelope.

And then he reached for the bottle of tequila.

When Annie woke up, she was disoriented. The bed sagged beneath her, the sheets were tangled around her legs, and the smell of frying bacon mixed with the rich scent of coffee. In the distance she could hear someone humming under his breath.

She felt exhausted, confused, hungover. She crawled out of bed, rummaged carelessly through her suitcase, and pulled out some clothes. By the time she reached the bottom of the stairs, she stopped in disbelief.

The tiny downstairs of the cottage was spotless. Gone were the dirty dishes she'd seen littering every available surface; gone were the stacks of newspapers and books, the clutter.

Gone was the stranger as well. McKinley stood in the kitchen by the stove, poking the bacon, sipping a mug of coffee.

He was showered, shaved, familiar again. He wasn't wearing a gray suit this time, and his hair was still long, but it was wet from his shower and combed back, and his clothes were neatly pressed khaki.

"There you are, sleepyhead," he greeted her, his voice an affable rumble, laced with his hint of Texas accent. "I thought you were going to sleep all day."

For a moment she didn't move, staring at him. In a way, this familiar James McKinley was even more startling.

"You want some coffee?" he continued, smiling an easy smile.

"Sure," she said after a moment.

"Take a seat. Breakfast is coming right up. Can't start the day without a decent breakfast," he said, turning away from her and whistling under his breath once more.

She waited until she gulped down a half cup of strong black coffee. She waited until he sat down opposite her, with plates of cholesterol between them. "What's going on, James?"

He didn't meet her eyes, simply busied himself with his breakfast. "I'm afraid you caught me at a bad time last night, Annie. You're probably not aware of this, but I have a drinking problem. I'm pretty damned good at covering it up, but there are times it gets the better of me. You happened to show up just as I was coming off a binge."

She stared at him. "I'm sorry. I had no idea."

"No, I'm pretty good at compensating," he said easily. "I've tried everything in the last twenty years, and I thought I'd gotten it pretty much under control, but Win's death hit me pretty hard."

"You've been an alcoholic for twenty years?" she asked, suddenly wary.

"For want of a better term," he said. "Your father tried to help me. He was a good man, Annie. One of the best. But there's nothing we can do to bring him back."

She stared at him, blinking for a moment, wondering what it was she was seeing. His skin was tanned, taut across the sharp bones of his face. There was no pouchiness, no sign of dissipation. "You don't think he was murdered?" she said carefully.

"No, I don't. Why would anyone want to kill Win? Everyone loved him. It was a freak accident, Annie. You know it as well as I do."

He made the mistake of meeting her gaze then. His eyes were clear. And they were the eyes of the dangerous stranger she had met last night.

What little appetite Annie possessed vanished. She'd wanted to believe last night had been an aberration, a combination of her exhausted paranoia and his unexpected drunkenness. She'd wanted him to tell her everything was all right, she'd imagined everything.

Doubtless that was exactly what he would tell her. The only problem was, she wouldn't believe him. Not after looking into his hollow eyes.

"Why aren't you working, James?" she asked quietly.

"I took a leave of absence. Mid-life crisis and all that," he said, his eyes not matching his self-deprecating voice.

"Then why couldn't I find any trace of you

when I tried to get your phone number? What happened to Win's tiny little sub-section of the State Department? Why was it disbanded when he died? Why isn't your name anywhere in the personnel records of the federal government when you've been working for them for as long as I've known you? What's going on, James? Why are you lying to me?"

He sat back, one large hand cradling his mug of coffee, his movements relaxed, measured. "You sure ask a lot of questions, Annie," he said finally. "I would have thought your daddy taught you the benefits of not being too damned curious."

"My father is dead," she shot back. "And I'm going to keep on asking questions, of anybody and everybody, until I find out some answers."

"I was afraid you were going to say that," he said gently. And from beneath the table he pulled out a gun.

She stared at it. It was large, blue-black, long-barreled, and fit comfortably in his hand. She looked at him, at the implacable expression on his face. The dangerous creature from the night before had vanished, but so had the gray-flannel bureaucrat she'd thought was James McKinley. This was someone else again. Someone who could kill her.

And then she laughed, a nervous reaction.

"God, James, what are you trying to do, scare me? I almost believed you for a moment. Why do you have a gun?"

He set the gun down on the table between them, carefully. "This is a dangerous part of the world, Annie."

"You probably don't even know how to use that thing."

"Don't count on it."

She bit her lip, frustrated. "You aren't going to answer my questions, are you?"

"I don't think you'd like the answers," he said.

"I'll get them from someone, sooner or later."

"Are you threatening me, Annie?" There was an undercurrent of amusement in his voice.

She lifted her head, meeting those strange eyes. "Maybe."

He sighed. "Okay."

"Okay, what?"

"Okay, ask me what you want," he said.

"Why couldn't I find any trace of you through the State Department? Why don't they have any record of your employment?"

"Maybe because I didn't work for the State Department."

"You worked with my father."

"Yes."

"Are you telling me my father didn't work for the State Department?"

"I'm not telling you anything. I'm just answering your questions."

"Who did you work for?"

"Ah, now that gets a little tricky. You're an intelligent woman, why don't you figure it out?" he suggested affably.

"CIA," she said, voicing her worst fear.

"Got it the first try."

"And my father?"

"He's the one who recruited me."

She just stared at him, sick. "You mean my father lied to me my entire life?"

"It's called need to know, Annie. It's not company policy to inform anyone unnecessary about our work."

"Anyone unnecessary?" she repeated as the slow tendrils of fury began to burn deep inside her. "Don't you think I had a right to know?"

"No."

"So what did the two of you do? Wander around the world like junior James Bonds?"

"You read too much, Annie. We were bureaucrats, plain and simple. The CIA has just as much paperwork as any other branch of the government—they just keep it more private. Your father was a policy maker, I was an accountant."

"An accountant," she said, looking at him

more clearly now. "Now, why do I have trouble believing that?"

"Maybe because you're in such a paranoid state you're imagining secrets everywhere."

"I'm finding secrets everywhere," she shot back. "I find that my father was a spook for the CIA, and his unremarkable best friend was a spy as well. How old are you? I asked you last night, and you refused to answer."

"Thirty-nine."

"Jesus," Annie said, staring at him. "How'd you get into this in the first place?"

"You mean, what's a nice guy like me doing in a job like this?" he countered blandly. "You know the details. Grew up in Texas, went to Harvard, got married, had a baby, and then my wife and child were killed in a car accident. I was at loose ends, and I didn't care much whether I lived or died. Your father brought me back. Gave me something to believe in."

"The Cold War," Annie supplied.

"For want of a better word. I'm not going to bother to explain it to you, or justify it. Things have changed in the last few years. Your father thought he was doing what was best for the world. Why don't you leave it at that? Leave him to rest in peace?"

"Was he murdered?"

For a moment she didn't think he was going

to answer. "Maybe," he said finally. "It's possible."

"And you haven't done anything about it?"

"What do you expect me to do?"

"Something a little better than running away and drinking yourself into a stupor," she snapped. And then she looked down at the gun, lying between them. "You really do know how to use that thing, don't you?"

"Everybody in the CIA gets some weapons training, even the clerical workers."

She had no idea whether he was telling the truth or not, but it seemed reasonable. "Why did you finally decide to tell me all this?"

"Because it's perfectly clear you're not going to go away and forget about it. And I'm sick and tired of lying. I suppose you have as much right as anyone to know about your father."

"Big of you," she said. "Does Martin know the truth?" She couldn't keep the faint hurt note from her voice. She'd trusted Martin wholeheartedly. She'd been married to him for three years, had even considered going back to him. Somehow the thought that he'd been keeping secrets, even when they'd slept together, was a final betrayal.

"Your father recruited him as well."

She took the blow, hiding her reaction from the surprisingly observant eyes across from her. "So what are you going to do about it?"

"About what?"

"About my father's murder?"

"You don't even know for sure that he was murdered."

"I know," she said fiercely. She thumped her chest beneath the thin cotton shirt. "I know in my heart, and my brain. And you know it too, no matter how much you're trying to deny it."

"I'm not denying it."

"Will you help me find out the truth?"

He leaned back, and there was resignation and regret in his eyes. "You don't leave me much choice, do you, Annie?" And he picked up the gun.

Chapter Three

Annie stared at him for a long moment as he held the gun in one large, capable hand. She held her breath, feeling oddly disoriented. As if she had jet lag, when she hadn't crossed any time zones coming after James McKinley.

He knew how to use that gun. Beneath his newly reacquired businesslike demeanor was a man who was far more dangerous than she'd ever expected.

She forced herself to turn away from him, pouring another cup of the wickedly strong coffee, and when she looked back the gun was gone. She didn't know whether he carried it or he'd stashed it someplace, and she didn't want to find out. It was gone, and that was enough. The sight of a gun in James McKinley's hands unnerved her.

The silence was heavy and uncomfortable between them, and she forced herself to break it. "What are we going to do next?"

His lids drooped over those disconcerting eyes, and she could almost tell herself he was the old, safe, reliable James. "Let me think about it for a while," he said finally. "It's safe enough here for the time being, if no one but Martin knows you're here. We'll take it a day at a time. You can tell me what you know, what you suspect, every tiny, seemingly meaningless detail. About the missing print, about anything he might have said, done. Anything that seemed different, strange to you. And then I'll decide what we can do about it. Whether I think there's anything that can be accomplished."

"And if you decide that there isn't?" she asked in a sharp voice, not bothering to hide her irritation with his high-handed ways.

"Then you can go back home with your mind at ease."

"It's not that simple. What if I'm not willing to take your word for it? What if you decide he wasn't murdered, that nothing was going on?"

He leaned back, his expression still carefully bland. "That leaves us with a little problem, doesn't it?" he drawled. "Tell me something, Annie. Why did you come after me? Why didn't you get Martin to help you? The two of you have shared a lot more than we ever had."

"What do you mean by that?" she asked in a wary voice.

"Just what I asked. Why didn't you go to Martin for help?"

"I did."

"You asked him for help in finding who killed your father?"

"Not exactly." That was another change since Win had died, Annie thought. She was no longer adept with the polite, social lies. "I asked him to help me find you."

"Don't you think he would have helped you?"

"I don't know," she admitted. "Win always said that if something went wrong, I should come to you. That you would know the answers."

"Did he?" There was no way she could read the expression on his face. "And you still do what your father tells you, don't you, Annie."

It wasn't a question, and she wanted to lash out, to deny it. She glanced down at her rumpled T-shirt, shoved her tangled hair away from her makeup-free face, and met his gaze quite calmly. "You tell me, James," she said.

It was a mistake. As long as he kept his lids half-lowered, she could lull herself into thinking he was the safe, protective presence she was looking for. When his gaze met hers, all bets were off.

"Point well taken," he said after a moment's

perusal. "I presume you're not sleeping with Martin anymore."

She spilled her coffee. The cup was almost empty, but the black liquid spread across the spotless table like oil. Or blood. "What business is it of yours?"

"Everything connected to Win is my business if you expect me to find out why he was killed. When you sleep with your father's protégé, then it might have a bearing, even if he is your ex-husband."

"I thought *you* were my father's protégé."

"And you haven't slept with me."

Yet. The word, unspoken, danced through her mind. She wondered whether it went through his as well. "I want to know more than why my father was killed. I want to know who did it."

"And what will you do then?"

"Kill him."

James's smile was brief and cool. "You could try."

"Or you could."

"We need to make sure it wasn't an accident first."

"We both know it wasn't." She set her coffee cup back upright with meticulous care, mopping up the spilled liquid with a paper napkin. "You still haven't told me how you knew I was back with Martin."

She'd manage to startle him at last. "I didn't realize it was still going on."

"It isn't. How did you know?"

"I searched your purse," he said dispassionately. "I read the letters."

"Both of them?"

"Both of them. Win wrote that if anything happened you should come to me. Why did it take you so long?"

"I don't believe in precognition. And I didn't want to deal with it."

"But now you're ready to?"

"I want to know who killed him."

James stared at her for a long moment. "Are you willing to take the chance that that knowledge might kill you? Why don't you go back home and get married again? Have babies and spend the money Win left you and not think about the past?"

"Who do you suggest I marry? Martin? It didn't work the first time."

"Still looking for someone to arrange your life for you?" he said. "I don't give a shit who you marry. I'm just suggesting you're better off forgetting your holy crusade."

"It's not that easy."

"It never is," he said. "Are you willing to take the risk?"

"Yes," she said, not even hesitating. "What about you?"

His smile was far from warming. "I've already gone way past that, Annie." He leaned across the table, and she knew with sudden certainty that he was going to touch her. And she didn't want him to. She wasn't sure why, she was just positive she didn't want those hands on her.

She left the chair, knocking it over as she backed away from him, and then she realized he hadn't moved. He was simply watching her, as if he could read her mind, her senseless panic, and for some reason it amused him. "He's not worth dying for, Annie," he said with unexpected gentleness. "Let him go. Forget him."

"He was my father. I can't," she said, and the ache in her voice was close to tears.

"Then God help you," he said.

He didn't think he was going to be able to do it. He'd managed to sober himself up, shave and shower and pull on the last remnants of anonymity along with the neat khaki stashed in the back of his closet. He'd woken up full of plans to lull Annie Sutherland into a false security and then send her back to Martin. She wasn't his responsibility, and hadn't been in years. Martin could sleep with her again, protect her, and manage to convince her that this was all a delusion caused by strain and grief. That Win's last, cryptic letter full of unlikely fatherly admonitions had nothing to do with a knowledge of impending death.

He still couldn't figure out why the hell Martin had let her come after him. He'd never known Martin to do a thing that he didn't want to, and that wouldn't benefit him in the long run. Maybe he thought the sight of McKinley in all his alcoholic ruin would send Annie back into his arms, into his bed, where he could take proper care of her.

Or maybe not. Martin was still there, in the center of everything, and he had to know more than James could at this point. Maybe Martin needed him to protect her. Or to effect a flawless cover-up, as he had so many times over the years. He'd sent no message with Annie, and there was no way he could come right out and ask him. Not without risking too damned many people finding out.

He was on his own, at least for now. With an albatross around his neck, an albatross with too many questions. If only he could manage to convince her there was absolutely nothing to her suspicions.

But he couldn't bring it off. He'd already told Annie too damned much, and he couldn't use the excuse of too much tequila. He'd never let alcohol loosen his tongue before.

Something had snapped inside him when Win had died, and all his years of training had gone south. He looked at Annie Sutherland's angry eyes, and he wanted to tell her the truth.

He wasn't that far gone yet. He wouldn't tell her the truth, ever. Not even if it came time to kill her.

She was standing with her back against the wall, looking at him as if he were her worst nightmare. She had enough sense to realize that much, he thought grimly.

He'd been about to touch her, and that would have been a mistake for both of them. He wasn't quite sure what he would have done. Whether he would have hurt her. Closed forever those blue eyes that saw him far too clearly, whether she realized it or not.

Or whether he would have kissed her.

He couldn't remember when he'd last kissed anyone. It wasn't a usual part of his sexual repertoire, and he couldn't even remember wanting to. He wanted to kiss Annie Sutherland. Christ, he always had.

"I think I'll go for a walk," she said in that same breathless voice that couldn't quite hide her nervousness. She didn't want him to see it, and for some reason he was willing to let her think he didn't know how much he frightened her. "I need some fresh air."

"No," he said.

"Don't be ridiculous," she shot back instantly. "I'm not going to stay cooped up in this cottage while you decide whether I'm having paranoid delusions . . ."

"It's dangerous out there. If you want to go for a walk, I'll go with you, but I think that would defeat the purpose, don't you? If you just want to get away from me, then go back upstairs."

"Why should I want to get away from you?"

He smiled at her. She didn't seem reassured. "You tell me."

"I should never have come here," she said bitterly.

"Probably not," he agreed. "But it's a little too late to change things."

"I could leave."

"Not until I say you can go."

She stared at him in shock. "You can't keep me here."

"I can do anything I goddamn please. And if you really want to put a halt to this, to go back to Martin, you can do so with my enthusiastic cooperation. As soon as I'm convinced it's safe."

"Why wouldn't it be?"

"If someone killed your father, they wouldn't be very happy about the two of us being together. You started the paranoid delusions, Annie. You're going to have to humor me for the next few days until I decide just how crazy they are."

He could see the anger and frustration in her pale face, and he wondered just how far he could push her. Now wasn't the time to try it.

She moved away from the door, running a hand through her shapeless mop of hair. She was biting her nails, he noticed. That was a far cry from her usually perfect manicure. "Maybe I'll take a nap," she said with studied nonchalance. "You can sit here and drink coffee and brood."

"Fine," he said absently.

But he didn't brood. And he didn't drink his coffee straight. He poured tequila into it, just a bit at first, because he discovered his hands were shaking. He could hear her moving around upstairs, and he poured himself some more, hoping to force his brain to concentrate on what he had to do.

He could send Annie Sutherland back to Martin. Except that Martin had to have had a reason to send her there in the first place.

He could kill her. That might have been what Martin had in mind, but he didn't think so. Even in their unsentimental branch of the business, people didn't take killing their ex-wives in stride. And while he usually viewed killing with calm detachment, he wasn't sure he could be as machine-like with Win Sutherland's daughter.

Or he could do as she wanted. Find out why Win was killed. Find out who and what had gone wrong.

He knew the official reason Win had died. He'd gone rogue, playing games, setting up his own little army of black hats that kept the Cold War hopping, even in its waning days. He'd been responsible for the deaths of dozens of unsanctioned people, not to mention their own operatives. He'd done it out of malice, and he'd done it for money. He deserved to die, no question about it.

There were strict rules about their tiny, nameless subbranch dedicated to what they liked to call wet work. None of the operatives knew how many were involved, nor did they usually even know one another. For all James knew there could have been a small army of people trained to kill, as he was. Or there could have been a mere handful.

He'd met a few of his associates over the years. Most of them were dead now. But he was left alive. For now. It made a cruel kind of sense. Of all of them, he was the one who most deserved to die. Who most wanted to die.

And fate had dealt him a crushing blow. Instead of expiating his sins, he'd compounded them. After the first few jobs he hadn't asked questions, and Win hadn't offered information. There'd been assassins, pedophiles, dictators, and torturers, all of them falling beneath his talented hands. He'd gone on assuming they'd all deserved their fate.

But Win had lied to him. And he hadn't been alone in his little enterprise. The anonymous, powerful beings who ordered the execution might have thought killing Win had solved the problem, but James knew that it hadn't. There were others who'd taken up the slack. Others, who'd set Win up to be discovered.

He wanted those others. He couldn't remember wanting to kill before, but he wanted to kill them. If Win had to die, those others did too. And if he did what Annie wanted, went after the truth, he meant to make sure they did.

"General?" The secretary with the tight ass and the unlikely tits approached him. He'd hired her for that tight ass. Not that he ever expected to partake of it, or even wanted to. But it kept the men around him mesmerized, distracted, and he was a man who took every advantage he could. "Mr. Carew wants a meeting."

The General gave her his avuncular smile, one that fooled almost everyone. "You know my schedule better than I do, honey. Set something up. Tomorrow, maybe."

"He said it was urgent, sir."

"Everything's urgent to that little weasel," he said amiably. "I'm not in the mood to listen to his rantings. That's the problem with this government nowadays, sugar. Too many civilians trying to run the army."

He never called her by her name. He knew it, just as he knew everything about her, including her teenage shoplifting, her experimentation with cocaine, her sexual leanings, and the way she took her coffee. He knew far more about her than she would ever know about him, and it provided him with an endless source of amusement.

"Yes, sir," she said, hiding the grimace that always greeted one of his endearments. She thought he didn't notice. She didn't realize that if she failed to react, he'd stop calling her things like sweetheart.

"Tell him tomorrow afternoon," the General said, heading down the corridor. By tomorrow afternoon his own particular ass would be covered, McKinley and Sutherland's daughter would be dog meat, and Carew could fuss all he wanted. The General paused at the end of the hallway and glanced back at his long-suffering secretary. "Find out what he wants in the meantime, will you, sugar?"

Her eyes narrowed in faint dislike. "He said it had something to do with Winston Sutherland."

The General indulged himself with a faint chuckle. "I imagine it does. Tomorrow. Late."

Carew would shit a brick when he found out McKinley had been taken out. He wouldn't much like it that Sutherland's daughter had bought it as well, but with any luck the team would see to it that that particular piece of business was covered up. As long as the press didn't catch wind of it. They didn't give a fuck how many soldiers died, but let it be a female and they'd all bust a gut.

As far as the General was concerned, women and children were far more expendable than a good fighting man. But the world was full of sentimentalists.

This time tomorrow Carew would be having a temper tantrum, and the General would have everything under control. Everything he'd worked for. Everything Winston Sutherland had played with and jeopardized like a spoiled child.

But the General had taken care of Sutherland. And he'd take care of anyone or anything else that got in his way.

Including anyone who might know anything about the night Sutherland died.

*　　*　　*

There was only one bathroom in the tiny cottage, and that was downstairs. It was already getting dark, and Annie had put off descending that narrow flight of stairs for as long as she possibly could. She wasn't ready to face James again. Not until she got a firmer grip on her temper, on her misgivings.

But her body wasn't giving her any choice. There wasn't a sound coming from the ground floor of the cottage, and the murky twilight barely pierced the gloom of the now tidy rooms. When she came out of the bathroom, she looked around her, carefully, for signs of her reluctant host.

He was nowhere to be seen. There was no door to his bedroom, and for some reason she felt an urgent need to look inside. It looked like a monk's cell. Narrow bed, made with army-like precision. Some drill sergeant could bounce a quarter off it, Annie thought absently.

There was nothing else there. No books, no pictures, no personal possessions. Nothing to fill the days and weeks he'd been there. The place was empty, soulless.

The dishes were washed. She found a can of chili and heated it on the gas burner, aided by a few soggy crackers. She was sitting at the scrubbed table, eating her way through the unappetizing meal with dogged perseverance, when she heard a sound out on the porch.

Her panic was immediate. He'd told her it wasn't safe, and all sorts of horrific thoughts came to mind. Someone had followed her, some crazed assassin, and James was out there, lying in a pool of blood, an innocent victim destroyed by her feckless determination. The man who had killed her father was out there, she felt it with an intense paranoia that bordered on certainty. She could stay in the kitchen, hiding, until he came after her.

Or she could go face him herself.

She pushed away from the table silently. She heard the noise again, a faint scrape, a breath, perhaps even the telltale beating of a heart, just beyond the sagging screen door. She moved slowly, carefully, closer, focusing on the silhouetted figure. Tall, powerful-looking in the shadows, he was standing in the corner of the porch, looking out into the surrounding jungle, and she thought she might be able to make it past him, running, into the jungle.

And she knew she wasn't going to do it.

She needed to look her father's killer in the eye, even if it cost her her life. She needed to see what her father last saw, and the risk didn't matter. She moved toward the dark figure, completely silent, reaching out her hand—

A moment later she was slammed against the wall, so hard that her vision blurred, her breath left her body, and all she could feel was agonizing pain washing over her. She clawed at the creature that imprisoned her, at the arm that had shot out, the hand that manacled her neck, and she knew she was losing consciousness. She wouldn't see him. She would die before she knew who'd killed her father, and that defeat was more than she could stand. She summoned up one last surge of energy, kicking at him, and suddenly she was free.

The shock of it was almost worse than the attack. She collapsed on the rough porch flooring, holding her throat, gasping for breath, and her entire body prickled with sharp nettles of reaction.

When she looked up at the monster towering over her, when her eyes could finally focus, she saw James staring down at her with a total lack of compassion. "Don't ever sneak up on me," he said. He held out a hand to help her up. The hand that had clamped around her neck, cutting off oxygen, that had almost killed her.

"I thought you were the man who killed my father."

She expected to startle him. He showed no reaction whatsoever. "In which case, your search would be over before it even began."

She ignored his outstretched hand, using the wall of the house to steady herself as she struggled to her feet. "You almost killed me," she said.

"No. I don't deal in almosts."

He was drunk. Not stinking, falling down, blindingly drunk. Just as drunk as he was the night before, with that raw edge of fury released by the liquor, simmering just beneath the otherwise emotionless surface.

He must have read her mind. His mouth curved in a mocking smile. "Want a drink, Annie?"

"I told you—"

"I know what you told me. I know it's a pile of crap. Why wouldn't you drink?"

"I stopped when Win died. The thought of him drinking too much, falling down those stairs . . ." She let it trail off with a shudder.

"Well, then," he said, "it seems you can repeal your vow with a clean conscience. Win didn't die from a drunken accident, he was murdered. Have a drink." He held out an almost empty bottle of tequila.

"You're drunk," she said in disgust.

"Just enough," he agreed.

"I'm getting out of here. You're of no earthly

use to me or anyone else. It's no wonder they just let you go." She started away from him, toward the steps.

How could she have forgotten, in a matter of moments, just how strong and fast he could be? He caught her, whipping her back, and she stumbled against him. Given the amount he'd had to drink, she would have thought she'd unbalance him, but he stood firm and solid as a rock. "I told you, it's not safe," he said in a harsh voice.

"And I'm safer with you? In your condition?"

"What do you think I'm going to do, Annie? Rape you?" It was a taunt. It should have seemed absurd. But it didn't.

She ignored the suggestion. "You certainly aren't in any shape to protect me from these nebulous dangers you keep trying to convince me exist."

"Annie, no one's going to take you from me if I'm not willing to let you go."

Again that strange undercurrent in his husky, faintly Texas voice. For some reason she thought of Martin, not some faceless villain taking her away. But James hadn't been talking about sex, had he? He'd been talking about life and death.

"I've decided to go back home," she said. "I'll talk to Martin and maybe he can do a few discreet inquiries. Just to set my mind at ease."

"Fine," he said. "But you're not going tonight."

She was leaning against his body, she realized suddenly. She could feel the smooth, muscled warmth of him beneath the now rumpled khaki. The heat, the steady beat of his heart. It was the steadiness of his heartbeat that convinced her. If it had been racing, she would have run, and the hell with the consequences. But he was obviously completely calm and in control despite the tequila he'd drunk.

And then he stepped back, away from her, and she felt light-headed. He stood between her and escape, a deliberate move on his part, and tipped the contents of the bottle down his throat. And then he looked at her.

"Go back to bed, Annie," he said. "We'll figure out what to do tomorrow."

"Tomorrow I'm going back to Washington."

"Fine," he said again. "In the meantime, why don't you go disappear?"

"Why?" Now that he was letting her leave, she stubbornly wanted to stay put.

"Because, as you've already pointed out, I'm drunk. And I've been here for three months, alone. And while you're not my type, at this point I'm willing to overlook that fact. So either go upstairs and keep away from me, or take off your pants."

She didn't hit him. She wasn't exactly sure why. Maybe because she knew he'd hit her back. Or because touching him, even in anger, might ignite something that was even more terrifying than the specter of death.

Or maybe because she suspected he was deliberately trying to intimidate her.

It didn't matter. She backed away from him slowly, and he let her go. "Are you ever going to tell me the truth?" she asked him, pausing by the door.

"About what?"

"Anything at all."

It was odd, the strange sense of yearning that sparked between them. A moment later it was gone, and he lounged against the railing, watching her coolly. "I doubt it, Annie. I doubt it."

Chapter Four

Annie came downstairs the next morning, wary, obviously expecting him to jump her. He'd managed to pull James McKinley back around him once more, and if he had more of a hangover than he wanted to admit, he figured it was his just punishment. She stared at him for a moment, uncertain.

She wasn't dressed in her traveling clothes, he noticed with a mix of admiration and despair. She didn't look the slightest bit terrorized. Just very careful.

"I thought I'd managed to convince you to run away," he greeted her.

"Why would you want to do that?"

"You're better off getting on with your life. It can be a dangerous thing, rattling cages."

"I don't think I have any choice," she said. "I can't let it go."

He sighed. He was going to have to cut his hair. He'd already shaved twice in the past two days, and the old reflexes were coming back. He was going to have to make up his mind. He'd come up with two possible solutions during the long, sleepless night. He just wasn't sure which one he was going to implement.

"I figured you wouldn't," he said pleasantly. "Which doesn't leave me with much choice, does it?"

"Does it?"

There were three of them out there. She hadn't the faintest idea, but James had counted them with uncanny accuracy. They'd gotten here faster than he would have expected. It was nice to know that the cessation of the Cold War hadn't blunted their abilities.

It had been a simple enough matter to get rid of the first one who'd come after him. He was young, new to the business, and he'd come alone. He had been no match for a man of James's skills. There were no witnesses, and the ocean was nearby.

But this time there would be a witness. A civilian, an innocent. Annie Sutherland watched him out of her clear eyes, totally unaware of the danger surrounding them.

They would take her out as well if they could, he knew that. Simply because they had the same training he had, and it was exactly what he would have done if the situation were reversed.

He moved to the cabinet over the gas burner and took out his 9mm, sliding back the bolt to make sure it was ready. It was the least innocuous of the weapons he had stashed around the place, and only the second most lethal. After his hands.

"What are you doing?" she asked, eyeing the gun warily.

She still didn't have a clue, thank God. "Going for a walk," he said, rising and tucking the gun in his belt.

"We haven't finished talking."

Her father wasn't the only one good at manipulating. "Listen," he said with just the right amount of weariness, "I've got a hangover and a short temper. Let me get some fresh air, think about things. I have an idea or two. When I come back, we'll talk."

"Does that mean you'll help me?"

"That means I'll think about it. In the meantime, why don't you take a long, cool shower? You look a bit battered."

Actually she looked hot, tired, grumpy, and delicious. Too long without a woman, James reminded himself again. He half expected her to flush, but Win's daughter seemed devoid of vanity. She simply shoved a hand through her hair and made a face. "I'm not surprised. I wouldn't exactly call this a luxurious vacation spot."

She was used to luxurious vacation spots, he thought sourly. With Win's handpicked escorts. "Take your time in the shower," he said with an affability he was far from feeling. "I won't be back for about an hour." He didn't want to lay it on too thick. The shower was in the middle of the house. She'd be safer there than any place else, and the sound of the water might drown out the noise of gunshots. His Beretta was equipped with a silencer, but even the top of the line was pathetically noisy. He'd have to work fast and hope she wouldn't notice.

He stepped off the porch, surveying the tropical morning as he listened to her moving around. He lit a cigarette, taking a deep breath of the ocean air, the subtle scent of foreign sweat on the breeze, as he waited for the sound of the shower. He figured he had ten minutes at worst, up to twenty if he was real lucky. In the old days he could take three operatives out in less than half that time. But this wasn't the old days, and he was feeling tired and angry. Emotions always slowed him down.

Another day in paradise, he thought sourly, taking a deep drag off his cigarette. He could hear the birds in the distance, edgy and disturbed by the presence of strangers. The hush of the ocean surf penetrated through the thick, jungle-like underbrush. There were a hundred places a man could hide in an overgrown place like this. And he felt a brief flash of that hateful, seductive anticipation.

He found the first one behind the house, his gun drawn, sneaking up toward the back porch. James came up behind him and broke his neck, quickly, efficiently, letting the body drop with a silent thud onto the soft, spongy ground.

Two left, he thought with clinical detachment, moving around the side of the house. The first one had been too easy. The next intruder was more of a challenge, staying just out of reach.

He was moving toward the house, James realized with only a brief moment of concern. No matter how good the operative was, he wouldn't be able to get to Annie. He'd have to come out in the open if he wanted to enter the cabin, and James could pick him off with a single shot.

The attack team might have brought a short-fused explosive device. Then they'd have to run like hell, and James had little doubt he could take them out and defuse whatever little present the company had come up with for one of their own.

At least his compatriots, perfectionists and professionals though they were, had never gone in for suicide missions. Staying alive had always been more important than getting the job done. Too bad this latest batch would accomplish neither objective.

There was only one slight difficulty. He still hadn't figured out where the third operative was.

His quarry made the mistake of stopping his determined advance toward the cabin. James found him squatting in the bushes about ten yards from the front porch, loading extra 9mm clips with hollow-point bullets. If it hadn't been for the bullets James might have considered letting him go, but those bullets were meant to maim and hurt. The man must have sensed his presence. He looked up, and there was a flash of recognition between the two. James had never seen him before in his life. But he knew him, as well as he knew himself. He shot him at point-blank range.

One left. He'd tossed his cigarette, and he could smell the coppery scent of blood, the iron smell of death on the air. And something else, something he recognized.

"Fuck me," he muttered.

"Not this time, James."

He turned, slowly, to face the third and final operative they'd sent after him. Mary Margaret Hanover. A woman with the face of an angel and the soul of . . . hell, she didn't have a soul.

"You've been your usual efficient self, James," she said coolly, moving around him with extreme care, her gun pointed directly at his crotch. "I would have expected no less. I tried to warn the others, but they seemed to think you were merely human. I know better."

"You going to kill me, Mary Margaret?" he inquired casually.

"Certainly. I'll regret it, of course, but I won't even hesitate. I'm following orders. Nothing personal, James. We've had some good times together, but I take my work seriously. Trust me, I won't enjoy killing you."

"That's a shame," he murmured. "You usually get off on it."

Her pleasant smile faltered for a moment. "Don't worry about me, James. After I take care of you, I get the little girl in the shower. I'll enjoy doing her, trust me on that one."

"You know who she is?"

"You think I'm sentimental about Win? I'm no more sentimental than you are, James. I do what needs to be done. With more pleasure than you've ever shown in your craft. Though in your case I might even call it sheer artistry."

"Do you have any regrets, Mary Margaret?" he asked gently.

Her smile was wide, innocent, bone-chilling. "None, darling. You're fiendishly inventive in bed, you're a brilliant tactician, but you've always been a little too moral for your own good. If you'd known the scope of the operation, you would have been tiresomely difficult. It was just as well most of us didn't even know each other and what we were assigned to do. But I can't regret knowing you, James." She smiled sweetly. "And your death will clean up a number of loose ends."

"Always glad to be of service, Mary Margaret. Just tell me one thing. Did you do Billy Arnett?"

"That sweet little yokel? He didn't belong in the company, James. He particularly had no business being groomed for our branch. Certainly he could shoot well enough to make even you look bad, but he was a child. A golly-gee-whiz patriot, for heaven's sake."

"Did you kill him?"

"Oh, that's right. He was your little protégé, wasn't he? You even set up some money for his wife. She was better off without him, you know. He slept with me, and he was lousy in bed. No staying power. Unlike you."

"Did you kill him?"

"Of course I did," she said irritably. "What has that to do with anything?"

Her cold blue eyes widened in sudden surprise. A second later the bullet hole appeared, in the middle of her forehead, and she crumpled onto the ground like a broken puppet. He stared down at her for a moment before lowering the gun. "Everything," he said in a soft voice. And then he stepped over her body and headed back to the house.

Battered, Annie thought as she stood under the shower, lathering her hair. It shouldn't bother her, but it did. It had nothing to do with James McKinley, she told herself, letting the lukewarm water sluice over her face. She didn't particularly want anyone thinking she looked the worse for wear. Win had instilled in her all sorts of priorities, and always facing the world well groomed and in control was part of it.

Funny, but right now good grooming seemed the least of her worries. In the months since Win's death she'd gradually stopped wearing the well-cut, pastel suits that took up most of her closet space. She'd given up her weekly manicure appointment, her hair was months past its usual careful shaping, and yesterday was the first time she'd worn heels in what seemed like centuries.

She had certainly picked the worst possible time to wear them. She was half tempted to throw them in the trash before she ever tortured her feet again.

She heard the sound when she stepped from the shower. A muffled explosion, and for some odd reason she thought she'd heard the same sound earlier, drowned out by the heavy water beating down on her head. She paused, listening, but there was nothing at all. Just silence.

She dressed swiftly, scarcely bothering to towel herself dry. Battered, he'd said. She deliberately refused to look in the mirror. She had no reason to pretty herself up for James McKinley. No need to drape herself in the bland, pretty clothes her father had approved of for her.

The flash of guilt was immediate. Her father had loved her, wanted the best for her. He was a connoisseur, an expert in matters of taste and art. He knew far better than she did what clothes and colors would suit her, what wine she would prefer to drink, what car she would prefer to drive. It didn't matter that deep in her heart she'd always longed for a gaudy, classic Corvette. She drove a late-model Mercedes. A perfect, elegant car that suited the person she knew herself to be.

She dressed in wrinkled white pants and a fuchsia silk T-shirt. She'd never worn fuchsia—it was too bright, too conspicuous, but she'd bought it anyway, then stuffed it in the back of her closet and forgotten about it. She brought it with her at the last minute, throwing it into her suitcase, and right now she was feeling defiant. No one could look battered in fuchsia.

She didn't see him at first when she emerged from the bathroom. He was sitting at the table, a cup of coffee in his hand. He looked cool, relaxed, a man at peace with himself. She almost envied that peace. Except for some reason she wasn't certain she believed it.

"I didn't realize you were back," she said, shoving a hand through her wet, tangled hair.

"It didn't take as long as I expected," he said.

"What didn't?"

"Deciding what to do." He took a sip of coffee. "Why don't you go upstairs and pack?"

"Am I going someplace?"

"We both are. I've decided to help you. If you still want me to."

"I still want you to," she said. "Where are we going?"

"All in good time, Annie. You're going to have to trust me on this. You're going to have to keep trusting me."

She hesitated, considering it. "All right," she said finally.

"It's that easy?"

"Don't you trust anyone?"

"Not a living soul."

She shook her head. "You must have a very empty life, James."

His grin was cool and savage. "You don't know the half of it, Annie."

He sat back, listening to her slam around upstairs, expressing her irritation with him in none-too-subtle ways. He smiled wryly. She never would have shown irritation while Win was still alive. He'd taught her that good manners were of paramount importance, and image was everything. One always had to appear in control of oneself, and one's situation, even if it was all a sham.

In Win's case it hadn't been. He'd controlled everything and everybody who came within his sphere, up until the last day of his life. James had accepted that unpalatable truth in the last few months, a truth he'd managed to avoid while Win was alive.

He'd left his mark on everyone, and it was only now, after his death, that they were beginning to emerge from his shadow. Martin Paulsen, Win's dutiful protégé, handpicked to marry his daughter, a clever, loyal, honest soul. Carew, the slimy excuse for a superior who'd finally gotten the last word, and no longer had to worry about Win looking down his patrician nose at him. Annie, wearing gaudy colors, glaring at him, slamming around.

And even James McKinley himself. He was

emerging from the shadows whether he wanted to or not. Coming out into the open, where he was a living, breathing target for the people someone, maybe Carew, sent after him.

They would keep coming, of course. Next time it might be a full-scale attack force of navy Seals, if they could come up with a believable excuse.

But there wasn't going to be a next time. He'd waited long enough for them to come and get him. They didn't let people retire in his line of work, not with his history. But he was tired of their inept attempts at taking him out. Of not knowing who or what was after him. He was going to bring the war right back to them.

But first he had a decision to make. If he had any sense at all, he was going to have to finish what he'd started. He was going to go upstairs and kill Winston Sutherland's daughter.

He'd known, as he'd dragged Mary Margaret's body into the bushes, that he really had no choice in the matter. He could get her away from this place without noticing the carnage that surrounded them, but sooner or later it would catch up with them. And to keep her alive would only complicate matters.

She served no useful purpose, and he had

been taught a ruthless efficiency. She was a complication, in his way, and the only obvious choice was to dispense with her.

The alternative was unthinkable. He had no reason to let her live, except for sentiment. Emotion. Old memories, a passing fondness he'd once had for a young girl, a moment in an empty house one Thanksgiving years ago when she was young and alone and he'd let his guard down for a brief while. She seemed to have forgotten, but it might come back to her sooner or later. And he couldn't afford to let that happen.

She was already doomed. Her parentage, and her curiosity, had made that certain. He could be gentle with her. Make it fast, painless. If someone was going to kill Annie Sutherland, then it ought to be him.

It wasn't as if he had a conscience that could bother him. He'd killed. He was good at it, neat and painless, delivering death to the deserving without pause or regret.

Or if the regrets had come, it had simply been part of his penance. The price he had to pay, to live out his life expiating his sin by compounding them.

Catholic guilt. He'd always taunted himself with that, with the knowledge that his mother's faith had eaten its way into his heart and soul, into his very bones like a cancer.

That too was his penance.

He moved up the stairs silently. Adrenaline was still pumping through him, a natural side effect of the past half hour. His pulse was steady, and his hands were without a tremor. This was what he did best. Mary Margaret had called it artistry. He doubted if Annie would consider her corpse a masterpiece.

She had her back to him when he reached the top of the stairs. She was stuffing clothes into her suitcase, and her movements were fast, jerky, angry. She picked up those absurd high heels, held them for a moment, and then slammed them into the wastebasket in the corner. It tipped over beneath the weight of her throw, and she muttered a curse.

He moved closer, so close he could reach out and touch that slender neck beneath the damp fall of hair. She wouldn't know what happened. A moment of pressure, and she'd be dead before she hit the floor. He could catch her, carefully, and lay her out on the bed. He would close her eyes, and then maybe he'd even burn the place down around her, a funeral pyre. He found he didn't want people touching her, messing with her, after she was dead.

He just needed to lift his hand. She didn't know he was there, behind her, ready to strike, but if he hesitated much longer she'd turn and see him, and recognize her death in his face. It would frighten her, and he didn't want to do that. If he was going to do it, he needed to make it as easy, as painless, as possible.

His muscles clenched painfully. He lifted his hand, and his fingers brushed her wet hair.

She whirled around and glared at him. "You scared the hell out of me," she snapped. "You're as bad as Win, tiptoeing around and sneaking up on people. Is that part of your stock in trade? Junior Spooks on Parade?"

He laughed then, a rough, harsh sound, and he wondered how long it had been since he'd laughed. Maybe a decade or more. He dropped his hand to his side, flexing his coiled fingers. "You've got more sass than brains," he drawled, using his best Texas accent.

"That's saying a lot. I was Phi Beta Kappa at Georgetown University."

He found he was grinning. It almost felt as if the stiff lines in his face would crack from the unexpected amusement. "Annie," he said, "you're getting in over your head."

"I already am. What do you suggest I do about it? Run away and hide?"

There was no place she could run to, no place she'd be safe. He knew that, even if she didn't. The safest place for her was with him. The man who had almost killed her.

He wasn't going to do it. Not now, at least, not while he had a choice. He knew enough about life to know that the damnedest things could happen. The odds were against the two of them, and if he were a gambling man he'd bet they'd both be dead by Halloween.

But odds didn't mean diddly squat when you threw human beings into the equation. She just might make it out alive. And if there was a chance, then he was going to see to it that she did.

He wasn't any too happy with his decision. It was impractical, emotional, a weakness. But when it came right down to it, he didn't want to kill Annie Sutherland unless he had to.

He reached past her for her suitcase, being very careful not to brush against her body. Her hair was already beginning to dry in the late morning heat, and he could smell the scent of her body, the heat of her skin. And, on the sultry breeze, the tang of blood and death.

"We're getting out of here," he said. "Before anyone else comes after me."

"Someone's come after you?"

"An annoying woman named Annie Sutherland," he drawled. "I don't want to risk having your ex-husband show up as well."

"I thought Martin was your friend."

"He is. Or as close to a friend as I have."

"Where are we going?"

"Do you trust me?"

She looked up at the man who was going to kill her, tilting her head to one side as she considered it. Her eyes were a clear, limpid blue. The same color as her father's had been, though without Win's malice or guile. She wore no makeup today, but oddly enough she looked prettier without the protective coloration she usually wore. Her skin was soft, fresh, touched with natural color. Her eyelashes were thick and tawny, like her hair. Her wide mouth was full, pale, and there was a scattering of freckles across her unremarkable nose.

Jesus Christ, what was he doing, standing there thinking about her freckles?

"Can I?" she said.

He wanted to tell her the truth. He wanted to tell her to run like hell, to get away from him as fast as she could. But it would be a waste of time. If she tried to run away, he'd catch her. If he caught her, he'd hurt her. Lying was the only choice.

"Of course, darlin'," he drawled, letting the

Texas slip into his voice, knowing its usual disarming effect. "Your father trusted me, didn't he?"

"With his life," Annie said.

Poor choice of words. He didn't let his faint, sexy grin falter. "Then you can trust me as well. I've got a car parked down the road a ways. We'll have to go through the brush, but you look a little better dressed for it today." He glanced down at her sneakers. She could run in those if she had to. He could carry her, if need be.

"Okay," she said. "Let's go."

Her sudden acceptance brought all his usual suspicions into play. People weren't as straightforward, as honest, as trusting as Annie Sutherland seemed to be. She'd probably stick a knife in his back before they were halfway to the car.

Or at least she could try. If Mary Margaret Hanover couldn't take him, then Annie Sutherland wouldn't be able to either. He half hoped she'd go for him. Then he wouldn't have to think about it, wouldn't have to decide. It would tie matters up quite neatly.

But life wasn't made of neat packages. She followed him down the stairs, and while half of him was tempted to push her up against a wall and run his hands over her, to make sure she wasn't carrying a weapon, the other half knew the worst thing he could do was to touch her.

He headed out onto the front porch. There were three corpses out back there. If he just kept her going straight down the path that paralleled the ocean, she would never know what had gone on here this morning.

"Aren't you going to pack?" she demanded.

"Don't worry about me, Annie," he said, waiting for her. "I can take care of myself."

She shrugged, stepping off the porch. And then her perfect, freckled nose wrinkled in sudden distaste. "What's that smell?"

"There are some pretty rank tropical flowers growing around here. That's probably the blood lily you're smelling."

"Never heard of it."

"They're endangered."

"Good thing," Annie muttered. "Anyway, it smells more like a septic tank."

She was too damned observant. "There's that too," he said. "Are you going to stand around sniffing the toxic waste or are you coming with me?"

"I'm coming with you," she muttered. "Whether I want to or not, I trust you."

For some reason he didn't find that reassuring.

* * *

He had had the strangest expression on his face when he'd come up on her in the bedroom, Annie thought as she trudged along behind him, the tiny cottage receding in the distance. It had been dreamy, erotic, and oddly threatening, and it had taken all her force of mind to say something sharp.

It had vanished, that expression, and she'd let out her breath. It was only now, following him through the thick undergrowth, that she realized how unnerving it had been. His black, empty eyes staring down at her, his hand upraised.

Had he been about to make a pass at her? It was the only logical explanation, and she was experienced enough to recognize that part of the tension that stretched between them was probably sexual. She didn't want to remember thinking of James in a sexual light. She was much safer thinking of him as older, unthreatening, as she had for the past few years. For a while she'd even wondered if he was politely, discreetly gay, but then she'd decided he didn't have even that outlet.

For some reason it had been important to her to see James in an asexual light. Right now, looking at his strong back, she wondered how she'd ever managed to do it. Memories tugged at the back of her mind, things she wasn't ready to remember. She'd had no more than an adolescent crush on him, for heaven's sake, one she'd outgrown swiftly enough when she met a real man, an appropriate man for her. Even if it hadn't worked out, her marriage to Martin had been reasonable.

She looked ahead at James, and a stray shiver crept over her. She didn't want to remember. James was empty. Soulless. He was a machine, one of Win's making.

Once more she tried to shut off that disloyal thought. Those harsh judgments were creeping in when she least expected it, and no matter how vigilant she was in trying to wipe them out, they always trickled back, in new and disturbing form.

Her father hadn't been a saint, for God's sake. He'd been a clever, admittedly manipulative man, good at controlling his surroundings and making everyone dance to his tune. Annie had been his puppet, and so had James. But the puppet master was gone, the strings were cut. And she was still struggling to stay upright.

"James," she said. "Who do you think killed my father?"

She waited for him to deny it again. He kept walking, his gait smooth and graceful. "Someone he loved," he said finally. "No one else could've gotten close."

Annie sucked in her breath. Round one. "Do you think he knew?"

James glanced back over his shoulder. "Without a doubt," he said. And he walked on, head bent, shoulders taut.

Chapter Five

He didn't drink on the plane. She noticed that right off, though she had the tact not to mention it. Their seats were first-class, the liquor flowed freely, and James McKinley drank mineral water, without lime.

Annie was amazed at how efficiently he'd got them there. The hike to the car had been the worst part, what with mosquitoes ravaging her skin, that awful stink lingering in the air, overpowering the fresh ocean breeze. He hadn't allowed her to take her time, and it wasn't until she was safely buckled into the front seat of the plain gray sedan that her instincts came alive.

"What's back at the house?" she asked.

James had already started the car, and he pulled into the narrow, rutted road without glancing in either direction, driving too damned fast. He didn't answer her, but she saw him glance down at the clock on the dashboard.

"James."

"What?"

"What's back at the house?"

An explosion answered her question. The force of it shook the road, sending the car skittering sideways before James ruthlessly straightened it. He didn't waste a look at the billowing tower of smoke in the distance where his cottage had been.

Annie swallowed her shock. The cool efficiency of it was almost worse than the destruction, and she felt anxiety eating into her stomach. It took her a moment to speak.

"Wasn't that a little extreme?" She managed to sound deceptively wry.

"No," James said. After an endless moment he continued. "There's always the remote possibility that they'll think we died in the explosion. At least it'll slow them down for a while."

"What are you talking about? Slow who down?"

He did turn to look at her then, and she almost wished he hadn't. "The people who killed your father. Isn't that what this is all about? You said you wanted to find out. You put yourself right in the middle of it when you came down to find me, and now there's no backing out. This is the way the game is played, Annie. Time to grow up and face the music."

"I don't feel like dancing."

"It's a funeral dirge."

After that she hadn't said a word. They'd taken a small boat off the island, and he'd handled it with the same cool dexterity with which he did everything, and she'd followed him blindly.

This was the third plane they'd been on that day. He'd paid for this one with an American Express gold card under a name she'd never heard before. She'd said nothing.

But now, as they flew into the sunset, she took a glass of cool champagne, downed it in one gulp, and stared at the man sitting next to her.

"Why are we flying west? I thought we were going to Washington. Last I knew, it was on the East Coast. Or has the CIA managed to change things around?"

"I'd watch my mouth if I were you," he said pleasantly enough, but there was no missing the light of warning in his eyes. "You never know who might be listening."

"I don't believe in your Cold War paranoia."

"You don't have to. You just have to do as I say."

"Where are we going?"

"To find the answers. We'll start in Los Angeles and go from there."

"Any particular reason for the detour? Or is

it just that three planes in one day aren't enough for you?" She reached out for the second glass of champagne, knowing she shouldn't do it. She was too tired, too edgy, too hungry to be scarfing down champagne.

"I like southern California."

"You always said you hated it. I remember you and Win bemoaning the fact that you were going to have spend three months there."

"You have too good a memory," he said casually. "I lied."

"When? Now or then?"

"All the time, Annie," he said gently. "All the time."

It took five glasses of champagne to put her to sleep. He was about ready to give her a little help—the CIA version of the Spock pinch—when she finally closed those damnably astute blue eyes of hers.

Damn, she was trouble. It didn't matter how tired she was, how much pressure he brought to bear. With Win's death the veil had been lifted, and she saw everything he didn't want her to see.

He could have used a little of that free champagne himself. Scratch that—he could have used a couple of bottles of the stuff, washed down with a fifth of tequila. He didn't dare touch anything harder than Pellegrino.

He was back in the real world now. On the island he had controlled his environment. No one could get close to him without him knowing. But now the cottage and at least a half dozen surrounding acres were toast, including all trace of his most recent visitors. And he had brought Annie out, into a danger he was no longer certain he could handle.

There was a piece of the puzzle missing, he was sure of it, but for the past few months he simply hadn't given a damn. He'd holed up, just waiting for them to send someone after him, and he'd kept his mind and his memories successfully dulled. He hadn't wanted to remember, not the night of April second, or the nagging questions that surrounded it.

He didn't want to think about how he'd got there in the first place. The organization, small, quiet, efficient, meting out justice and cleaning up political messes where overt organizations were helpless. He had done his share, never realizing he was part and parcel of making things worse.

All the tequila in Mexico couldn't burn that knowledge from his brain, and then Annie showed up, and all those questions flared into the open again.

Win Sutherland hadn't been alone. In his schemes, his tricks, his games. In his lucrative little sideline, ordering death for the right price and sending out his loyal minions. His stooges.

Carew might be fool enough to think the organization had stopped with Win's death. James knew better. Up to now he hadn't given a shit. Let them all keep killing one another. He was out of it, just waiting for someone good enough and fast enough to finish him.

But everything had changed. He wasn't through yet. He couldn't just let it go and let them sort things out, not with Annie poking her nose into things. He couldn't count on Martin to protect her—he was good, but he'd never done any wet work. As far as James knew, he probably couldn't even shoot a gun. He'd be no protection at all for those who'd come after Annie.

So he was back, whether he wanted to be or not. And this time he wasn't going to let go until he found the answers. He'd take Carew by his scrawny little throat and force him to tell him everything. Carew wanted him dead, just as Win's associates did. At least he could bargain with Carew for a cease-fire. Just long enough to find the answers.

What the hell was that stupid embroidery Annie kept yammering about? Probably a red herring, or maybe some kind of code. He wished he could just ignore it, concentrate on whom Win had seen last, where he'd been.

But he was good at his profession. And he knew he couldn't afford to discount anything, even some tacky "luck o' the Irish" wall hanging.

He needed answers, and he wasn't going to stop until he got them. Knowledge was power. Knowledge was control and a faint modicum of safety. He doubted he could buy his own safety, but he might be able to buy a life for the tart-tongued woman sleeping so soundly beside him. With luck, it just might be enough.

"We've got a problem, sir."

"So what the hell else is new?" the general snapped. It was early evening, but this time the office was far from deserted. The man standing opposite him had an ostensible reason for his visit, but one that wouldn't hold up to too much scrutiny. It had to be something pretty damned bad to get him over here. "You're going to tell me McKinley got away, aren't you? I don't want to hear it."

"I'm not sure. The place blew up, and we haven't been able to contact our operatives yet. With any luck Hanover will have set it and taken care of both of them."

"Who says we can expect luck in this business?" the General said sourly. "McKinley's an expert in explosives—better than Hanover ever was."

"Was, sir?"

"You may not be sure, son, but I am. Your people are gone. McKinley got away again, damn his eyes. And he probably took Sutherland's daughter with him. We're in deep shit, son."

"Yes, sir."

The General leaned back with a weary sigh. He was getting too old for this. It was time to think of more pleasant battles to be won. He had his future all nicely mapped out for himself. He'd start small—secretary of defense maybe. He knew how to twist arms, how to grease palms—he was a consummate politician as well as tactician, and he'd been working on his public image all his life. It was time for it to pay off. His lucrative sideline had gone bust—he was a smart man and he knew when it was time to cut his losses. There was the future to look forward to. He wouldn't settle for less than complete power. Preferably chief of staff. Or maybe the lesser job of president.

But he wasn't getting anywhere near the White House with a loose cannon like McKinley waiting to go off. He had to make sure there were no skeletons rattling in his closet.

And McKinley's bones were already making a hell of a racket.

"All right, son," he said heavily. "I'll take it from here."

The yuppie scum in his damned Italian suit and too long hair looked surprised. "Sir?"

He wouldn't have lasted a week in the old army. Of course, with the new one, chock-a-block full of women and faggots, he'd probably fit right in.

"I've got alternatives. You've failed, son. Time to let an old soldier take over."

He didn't like that, the General thought with cool amusement. But he knew there wasn't a blessed thing he could do about it. There were times, he thought, when life could still be sweet. And squashing an Ivy League dickhead was one of those moments.

"I'll have McKinley and the girl taken care of. Don't you worry your head about it," he added grandly. "You can stop wringing your hands."

"Sir?"

"Yes, son?"

"I wouldn't underestimate McKinley if I were you. They don't call him Dr. Death for nothing."

The General frowned. The boy didn't stay squashed for long. "I think you can count on me to handle him. I have resources unconnected to your little operation. McKinley won't be expecting it. As soon as I find out where he is, I'll have him and the girl taken out."

"If you say so, sir."

"You sound doubtful, son. Would you care to place a little bet?"

The man grimaced. "No, thank you, sir."

"Think it's in bad taste, do you, boy?"

"No, sir. I just don't make bets that I think I might lose."

The General leaned back, suddenly more in charity with the world. "You're a smart man. I'll keep that in mind."

"I'd appreciate that, sir."

Dickhead, the General thought genially as the door closed behind him. But a damned clever one at that.

He moved her through customs swiftly, and she stumbled after him, temporarily obedient, unable or unwilling to ask any more questions, put up any more arguments. He expected that if it had been up to her, she would have stayed asleep the moment the plane landed and let him cart her around over his shoulder.

But he would have put his hands on her, and that might have been a very big mistake for both of them. She was exhausted and not quite sober, and while he shared the first condition, he would have given anything to share the second.

Clancy was waiting for them at the prearranged spot, and the moment he caught sight of McKinley he started toward the exit, secure in the knowledge that they'd follow at a discreet distance. Annie didn't murmur more than a token protest when he put her in the backseat of an aging Toyota and then closed the door after her, taking the front seat beside Clancy. He could feel her glaring at the back of his head as they pulled into the pre-dawn traffic, and he glanced at her. "Go to sleep, Annie. Everything's under control."

She didn't say a word. She simply lay back and closed her eyes, but McKinley wasn't fooled. He had no doubt she would listen to every word they said.

Clancy kept his gaze glued to the road. "Who is she?"

McKinley considered his various answers. He was tired himself, and the memory of the brief, efficient blood bath that morning still lingered in the hidden recesses of his brain. Haunting him, as it always did. "Someone I'm sleeping with," he said in an offhand voice.

"I don't buy that. You never let your cock tell you what to do, and you wouldn't have brought her along unless you had a reason."

"You really want to know, Clancy?"

He watched Clancy consider it. He'd been in the business for more than ten years, but for the past three he'd been retired, providing occasional consulting services and living off his pension. Win had kept his operatives and their targets carefully segregated, but occasionally their paths would cross. James had run across Clancy in Panama, each on separate missions, sent by the same man. Both stained with blood.

Clancy had been the pragmatic one. It was a living, and none of the people he'd taken out was of any benefit to the world. They caused far more harm than good, and Clancy figured he was doing society a favor.

James couldn't see it quite so clearly. That Catholic guilt haunting him. The memory of a corpse-strewn square, and women crying, lingered in some dark part of his mind.

But for all Clancy's cool practicality, McKinley trusted him more than he trusted anyone else in this world. Which wasn't saying much, he thought sourly.

"No," Clancy said finally. "I guess I don't want to know the details."

"Where are we going?"

"I've got a safe house for you up in the hills. You've got it for as long as you need it." Clancy jerked his head toward Annie's reclining figure. "Is she one of us? Can we talk?"

"To some extent," he said evenly.

"Did you ever find out what happened to Win?"

She didn't make a sound, but he could practically feel her adrenaline kick in. "Not yet," he said.

"Think Carew knew about it?"

"Yes."

Clancy considered it for a moment, then nodded. "That's what I thought. Bastard."

"Yes."

"Any idea why?"

James didn't even consider telling him. Clancy lived with his choices, his life. He didn't need to know the truth about the filthy work he'd dedicated his life to. Didn't need to know that some of those targets had merely been someone's inconvenience, taken out for a price.

"I'm not going to ask you if you're going to do something about it," Clancy said. "I know you well enough to know the answer. I'm just offering my help if you need it."

"Clancy," he said wearily, "you've earned your rest."

"So have you, man."

"No rest for the wicked, Clancy."

Clancy hadn't lost his touch. The house was tiny, remote, up at the end of a narrow dirt road. Trees closed in around it on two sides, and the back overlooked a canyon, a cliff so steep and overgrown it would take a well-equipped army to maneuver up it. No one could get anywhere near the place without McKinley being aware of it, and he had no doubt Clancy had a sniper rifle set up for him to ward off any intruders.

Clancy didn't even turn off the engine when he pulled up to the vine-covered front door. "There's plenty of food and booze, and I took care of everything else you asked for. I'll call tonight and see what else you need."

"Did you set up the meeting?"

"Yeah. He wouldn't say when. You know Carew."

"I know Carew. Is the phone line clear?"

"It was last time I checked. With three relays set up so they can't trace you. Carew knows where you are, but no one else can find out unless he tells them."

"Maybe," he said. "You're a good man, Clancy."

"I wish I could do more."

McKinley slid out of the car, pausing by the back door. Annie had discovered that the Toyota came equipped with child-safety locks, and there was no way she could open the door herself. She wasn't a happy woman.

He didn't give her a chance to start arguing. He moved her out of the car and into the house, fast, before she could start yelling at him, and this time he had no choice but to touch her. He put his hand over her mouth, shoved her up against the door, and held her there, in the stillness of the darkened house, as he listened for sounds of intruders.

There was no one there now. He knew it, with a sureness he could never explain but had saved his life countless times. The place was empty, safe.

And then Annie quivered.

He looked down at her. Her wide blue eyes were staring up at him, and the anger that had burned there was gone. She looked shocked, dazed, vulnerable, and he knew it had nothing to do with death and her father, and everything to do with his body pressing up against hers in the small, dark hallway.

She felt hot, strong, alive against him, and he found he had this crazy urge to move his mouth down to the side of her neck, to press it against her, to taste her skin. He wanted to feel her breasts, wanted to pull her T-shirt up and feel her hot skin against his. Damn, he wanted her.

He released her, backing away before she could feel his immediate response. Clancy said he never used to think with his cock. Clancy didn't know that times had changed.

"What are we doing here?" she demanded in a shaky voice.

"Waiting for someone." He moved away, scouting out the tidy layout of the little bungalow. It was an old building, modeled after an English cottage, all multipaned windows and trailing rose bushes. He could smell the scent of roses in the air, and it gave him a sharp pang. The Sutherland house in Georgetown was surrounded by roses. There had been a vase of pink, fragrant ones in Win's study after the memorial service.

"Carew. Why? Do you think he knows who killed my father?"

"Probably. But he's not likely to volunteer that information."

Small living room, flowered wallpaper, chintz slipcovers, he noted. Working fireplace that would be perfect for hiding a bug. Alcove dining room and beyond that a small kitchen. He moved toward it, tossing his answer back over his shoulder.

"The man who killed your father doesn't matter," he said, pushing the swinging door inward. The kitchen hadn't been remodeled since the house was built, sometime in the twenties or thirties. He wondered whether Annie could cook.

"That's a matter of opinion." She was right behind him, too close, and if he backed up he'd run into her. He didn't want that to happen. "You still haven't told me what you expect to get from Carew."

He turned, his arm brushing against her breast. "A cease-fire. Maybe some information, though I doubt he'll be all that helpful. What I need from him is a promise to call off the dogs. To give me a week, two at the most, to find out . . ."

"To find out what?"

"To find out why your father was marked for death," he said finally.

"And you think Carew knows why?"

"He might. Since he was the one who gave the orders."

She stared at him, speechless in shock. "You knew that, and you did nothing about it?" she demanded, suddenly furious. "You heartless bastard, how could you let him get away with it . . . ?"

She made the mistake of touching him, as he knew she would. She caught his arms, trying to shake him in her rage, but he simply twisted his hands around hers, imprisoning her wrists. Making no effort to crush the fragile bones, as he could so easily. Simply holding her there, a prisoner. Enjoying it, damn his soul.

"Why do you think I was in Mexico, Annie?" he asked gently. "Carew wouldn't tell me a damned thing. I tried to kill the little prick. Twice. The second time no one really believed it was an accident, and I knew I wouldn't get a third chance for a while. And that they'd get me first."

"You said you were a bureaucrat. A pencil pusher. An accountant, for God's sake. You don't try to murder someone."

"I said I was an accountant for the CIA. For a small, obscure branch of it, and you'd better thank God it is obscure. You don't want to know about it."

"It was my father's work, wasn't it? I want to know."

"Tough. We'll wait for Carew."

"Are you going to try to kill him again?"

He considered the notion and found it, as always, appealing. "Maybe," he said after a moment. "Or maybe I'll just settle for a few answers and a short-term truce."

"You're crazy, you know that?"

"You were the one who came looking for answers. Have you changed your mind, Annie?" He almost hoped she'd say yes. It might be worth the risk, to send her off with Clancy and do the deal with Carew by himself. There was still the remote possibility that they didn't know she'd found him.

Yeah, and there was the remote possibility

that Jimmy Hoffa was alive and well and living in Fresno. He wouldn't bank on either one.

"No," she said, suddenly still and quiet. "I haven't changed my mind."

"You want answers?"

"Yes," she said. "And I want revenge."

She was, after all, Win's daughter. He looked down into her clear blue eyes, so like her father's. "Against Carew?"

"Against the man who killed him."

He simply nodded, releasing her, turning to check the contents of the small refrigerator. He already knew there'd be liquor in the cupboard, just as he knew there'd be weapons. Clancy was a thorough man, and he knew his taste in liquor and guns. "What do you intend to do about it? Once we find out for sure who did it, who gave the orders and who set him up. I could be wrong about Carew. I could be wrong about everything. What if it turns out to be someone you care about? A friend. Are you going to bring them to justice?"

"No," she said. "I'm going to kill them."

He kept his face in the coolness of the refrigerator, studying the bottles of Dos Equis for a moment. When he pulled back his expression was bland.

"You think you can do it?" he inquired in a perfectly reasonable tone of voice.

"After you failed? Yes. You see, he was my father. I loved him."

"You're forgetting something. He was like a father to me."

The notion clearly startled her. "Look," he said before she could protest, "why don't you go check out the bedrooms, maybe take a little nap? I don't know when Carew is going to show up, but . . ."

"What makes you think he will?"

He allowed himself a small, dangerous smile. "He'll be here," he said. "I can promise you that."

For a moment she looked uncertain. As if she still didn't quite know what to think of him. "All right," she said. "Maybe I will."

She turned from him, leaving the room, and he wondered briefly whether Clancy would have been careless enough to leave the weapons out. He doubted it. Training like Clancy's and his didn't go away no matter how long you were out of the business.

She looked deceptively strong from the back, with her sweep of hair and straight shoulders. He knew the truth, though, and it depressed him.

"Annie," he called after her.

She paused in the doorway, looking back at him. "Yes?"

"You're forgetting one thing. The man who killed your father. The man you want to kill."

"What about him?"

"He's going to try to kill you first. And he's a professional—he doesn't often make mistakes."

"How do you know that?"

"Just trust me. I know."

She nodded. "All right. I'll be ready. And you will too, James. Won't you?"

He nodded, trying to quiet the feeling of dread that lay like a burning stone in the empty center of him. "I'll be ready, Annie," he said very gently.

He waited until he heard her footsteps on the stairs. And then he turned to the cupboards, to the bottle of Jose Cuervo he knew he'd find there. Clancy always had a gift for details.

He broke the seal, unscrewed the cap, and poured a healthy dose down his throat, waiting for the familiar warmth to flood him.

It took a second swallow. He shuddered, setting the bottle out on the counter. And then he went in search of the weapons.

Chapter Six

There was only one bed upstairs. Two rooms, but one was used for storage. The other was almost nauseatingly cute—ruffled curtains at the multipaned windows, chintz bedspread, rag rugs on the floor. The bed was big enough for two or three, but Annie had no intention of sharing it with McKinley. No intention of sharing it with anyone.

She moved to the window, looking out over the canyon below. She'd never spent much time in California—it had always seemed too alien to her East Coast sensibilities. Win had always said that grown-ups didn't live in California, and Annie had agreed.

Now she wasn't quite sure why. Why she'd disliked California, why she'd blindly agreed with everything her father had decreed. Win had never seemed that overbearing. He'd influenced her through his gentle, mocking charm.

She pushed open the window, letting the soft breeze fill the room. She could smell the distant tang of wood smoke, and she wondered if Los Angeles was burning once more. She found she didn't really care.

She sat on the bed, kicking off her shoes. She was too tired to stay awake, too weary to sleep. She stretched out, trying to clear her mind of everything but the clear blue sky outside the window. All she could see was blood and death and danger.

If she fell asleep, maybe everything would be back to normal when she woke up. Maybe James would be the elderly cipher she'd conveniently thought him. Maybe her father would rest peacefully in his grave instead of haunting her, demanding revenge. Maybe she could find her safe, comfortable life once more.

She didn't think so. Life had shifted, changed irrevocably over the past six months, in ways she hadn't even realized. All culminating in the past forty-eight hours, with McKinley's paranoid fantasies of death and war.

She wanted it to go away. And it wouldn't take much to make that happen—she could simply put her shoes back on, go downstairs, and call a taxi. Tell James she'd changed her mind—she didn't want answers or revenge.

Because already she wasn't liking the answers she was getting. And revenge was a two-edged sword.

She lay on the bed, wide-eyed, sleepless. She could hear James moving almost soundlessly through the small house. The snick of metal as he fiddled with some kind of machinery in the adjoining storage room that looked out over the winding drive, the rustle of cloth, the scuff of shoes, a few distant thumps and thuds from the valley below. All familiar, normal sounds of life. All with sinister explanations.

She climbed off the bed, not bothering with her shoes, and crossed the small hallway. The door to the storage room was ajar, and she pushed it open, expecting to see James in there.

The room was empty. Just the boxes and covered furniture she'd discovered on her earlier foray. But now there was something else. A rifle was mounted on a tripod-type device, pointing out toward the road.

She stared at it with sick horror. He couldn't have brought it with him—customs had been rigorous, and they'd only brought out what they could carry from the seaside cottage. But the gun hadn't been set up an hour before. What was he planning to do with it? Surely he wasn't capable of using it?

"In case we get any unwanted visitors." His

voice came from directly behind her, answering her unvoiced question.

She turned. He was closer than she'd expected, and she controlled her tiny shiver of unease. "Do you know how to use that gun?"

"It's a sniper rifle," he said. "I could reel off the statistics, but I don't think it would mean much to you. And yes, I know how to use it."

He'd changed. He was wearing a black T-shirt and jeans, and his hair was wet. He looked lean and fit and dangerous. "I remember," she said. She saw the glitter in his eyes, and her misgivings grew. "Have you been drinking?"

"Not enough to notice. Don't worry, Annie, I'll keep the bogey man away."

"But what if you're the bogey man?"

The words surprised her, but even more shocking was their effect on James. He looked as if he'd been punched in the stomach.

He recovered so quickly she almost thought she'd imagined his reaction. "You're right, Annie. Don't trust anyone. Even me," he said.

"Don't be ridiculous. You're not going to hurt me," she scoffed, believing it. "You wouldn't have made sure I got safely out of Mexico. You wouldn't have brought me here if you were going to hurt me. And why should you?"

"Because you're asking dangerous questions. You're sticking your nose in places better left alone, and sooner or later you're going to uncover something that could make a very big mess indeed. It would only make sense for me to shut you up before you caused some permanent damage."

"Shut me up? How? I'm not easy to silence."

"Certainly you are," he said, his voice shot with silk. He slid his hand alongside her neck, under her fall of hair, his fingertips stroking the sensitive skin beneath her ear. She could feel her pulse leap beneath his flesh, and there was nothing she could do to stop it. "All it would take would be a measured amount of pressure. Deftly applied, at just the right spot, and presto—no more problems."

"You think you could knock me out that easily," she said, swallowing her spurt of fear.

"No, Annie. I could kill you just that easily," he replied.

She was trembling, and she hoped to God he couldn't feel it. "Why would you want to do that?"

"Maybe I'm the man who killed your father."

She couldn't move. She was mesmerized by him, by the bleak intensity in his eyes, the heat and strength of his body, the sheer force of his presence. He overwhelmed her, frightened her, and it took all her concentration to laugh, to break the thrall of sex and violence he'd held her in.

"Don't be ridiculous, James," she scoffed, moving away from him, from the touch of his hand, from the glitter in his eyes. "You loved Win as much as I did, we both know it. Don't bother denying it."

"I wouldn't. It's true."

She shook her head. "You know, I don't know if I believe anything you tell me. You're probably no more capable of killing someone than I am. You're just trying to convince me we have a chance in hell against . . . against the people who killed Win."

"And are you convinced, Annie?"

She looked up at him, at the dark, soulless eyes that had once seemed so cool and unthreatening. "Yes," she said quietly. "I am."

"Good." He moved past her to stare out at the winding road, resting one hand on the rifle. It was a possessive hand, almost like a lover's caress, and she felt a stray shiver dance across her backbone. "You want something to eat?" he asked casually.

"I'm not hungry."

"If I were you I'd eat," he said. "You might need every advantage you can get."

He had long fingers, narrow, deft-looking. Neatly trimmed nails, strong, elegant wrists. They were beautiful hands, and he stroked the cold metal of the gun absently, with an erotic grace that left her feeling sick. And oddly disturbed in ways she refused to define.

She wanted to slap his hand away from the gun. She wanted to leave the room, run away. Instead she was mesmerized, staring, unable to help herself. "How long will we stay here?" she asked, striving for normalcy.

"As long as we need to. Until Carew comes and we figure out where to go from here." He turned to look at her, and with a mere blink he took in her fascinated gaze.

He dropped his hand from the gun, not self-consciously, and tucked it in his pocket. "If you're not hungry, I am, Annie," he said gently. "It probably wasn't wise for me to drink on an empty stomach and no sleep."

It galvanized her as nothing else would. "I'll make us something," she said grudgingly. "But I know you're trying to manipulate me. Don't think you can get away with it."

"Why not? Win always did."

She slammed the door on him. The loud crash was mildly satisfying, though she couldn't stomp down the narrow stairs effectively in bare feet. The bottle of tequila stood out on the counter, and at least a third of it was gone.

Sudden apprehension washed over her. She took the bottle over to the old iron sink and poured the rest of the contents down the drain. The acrid stench of alcohol filled the room, and she knew a moment's misgiving.

She shoved it down. She was damned if she was going to put her life in the hands of a desk-bound CIA agent with cowboy fantasies and let him fuel those fantasies with too much alcohol. She had yet to decide just how real the danger was. But until she did, she wasn't taking any chances. James McKinley was going on the wagon, whether he wanted to or not.

Annie made scrambled eggs from the limited contents of the refrigerator. She called up to James, but he didn't answer, so she sat and ate hers, dutifully, watching as his grew cold and jellied on the plate.

She found him asleep on the bed, his long, black-clad figure stretched out across the coverlet. He'd closed the windows, and the room was stuffy. She stared down at him for a long moment, seeing him for the first time without the distraction of his looking back at her.

He was taller than she'd ever realized. Lying angled across the huge bed, he filled it. He had the body of a high jumper—long, rangy muscles, long bones, sinewy and strong. His damp hair had dried, curling slightly at the back of his neck, and it was dark brown mixed with gray. Slightly thin at the very back of his head.

For a moment she smiled, the one imperfection making him somehow more human. He shifted in his sleep, rolling onto his back, and she looked at his face. The lines were scored deep, around his eyes, bracketing his mouth, visible even in sleep. Those lines hadn't come from smiling. It was no wonder she'd always thought he was much older. For all that his face and body were in their late thirties, his heart and soul were ancient.

And the thought came to her, out of nowhere. What in God's name had Win done to him?

She wanted to touch him. Some small, mad part of her wanted to climb up on that bed and soothe away the lines that marred his face, even in sleep. He should look innocent, boyish as he slept. Instead he looked like a soldier in Death's army.

She backed away, quickly, before she could give in to the temptation. What the hell was wrong with her? James McKinley wasn't a man to be touched, to be stroked, like a stray kitten. He was a dangerous man—she was coming to realize that more and more, as unlikely as the notion had first seemed.

Too dangerous for her. She'd been a fool to come after him, a fool to ask him for help.

Even beyond the grave Win was manipulating her, and by now she should have had enough of it.

She grabbed her shoes, closing the door silently behind her as she tiptoed down the stairs. He would sleep for hours. She'd leave him a note, apologize for stirring things up, and get the hell out of there. By the time he awoke she could be halfway back to Washington. Back to Win's house, surrounded by the artifacts of Win's life. Everything but the silver-framed print of the Irish saint. Back where she belonged.

The note was brief, scribbled on a pad of paper. She left it next to the empty tequila bottle, grabbed her purse, and stepped out into the hot California sunshine. There was no car—Clancy had said he'd return some time that evening, but Annie figured it would take her about fifteen minutes to hike out to the highway. Then she'd take her chances on hitchhiking back to the city, to public transportation of some sort that could get her to LAX. For some reason hitchhiking seemed safer than waiting in that little house with the man asleep upstairs.

She was halfway up the winding drive when she smelled that awful smell. What had James called it—the blood lily? It smelled like septic tanks and blood. It smelled like death.

She stopped in the middle of the driveway, riveted, as that hideous, unwelcome thought squirreled its way into her brain like a hungry maggot digging into dead flesh. Death and carnage. She looked up, toward a hawk wheeling and turning overhead. It wasn't a hawk. It was a vulture.

She wanted to turn and run. But she had no idea where she could run. James was back at the house with his knowledge of weapons and the secrets in his cool, merciless eyes. There was no safety back there. Ahead of her lay death.

She forced herself to look around her. She couldn't rid herself of the eerie notion that she was being watched, even though she knew she was being ridiculous. Who would be watching her? James was dead to the world in that big bed upstairs, and there was no one in sight, no one who could be watching her, no one knew they were there, or would even care. She was alone in the brilliant California sunshine, with only the vulture for company.

She took a deep, calming breath. She was overwrought, overtired, jumping at shadows. She simply needed to keep walking, putting one foot ahead of the other, until she made it out to the main road. There was no danger, no death around her. It was a bright day in California, the sunshine state.

She managed to move, forcing herself, down the dusty, rutted driveway. From a distance she could see a flash of light, the sun bouncing its reflection against a shiny surface, and once more she halted, squinting into the undergrowth.

And then she saw a car.

She should have kept going. Past the telltale section of undergrowth. But she couldn't help it. She took one step closer, then another, as she recognized the battered silver-blue of the Toyota Clancy had picked them up in.

The car had to be empty. He must have driven off the road and then gone for help. Except that there were no signs of an accident. The car had been driven there, hidden there, with great care.

She pushed the bushes aside, assailed by the stench. There was nothing resembling a lily anywhere around, and yet the too familiar smell assaulted her.

The car wasn't empty after all. She could see his shoulders slumped over the steering wheel. See the smear of blood on the cracked windshield.

There was no reason to move closer. She knew immediately that he was dead—the back of his head had been blown away. She stumbled backward, a scream bubbling up in the back of her throat. But no sound came out, nothing but a faint, gasping noise, as she struggled for breath.

An arm snaked around her throat, hauling her back with a rough jerk, cutting off her already desperate attempts to breathe. Horror erupted, and she fought, insanely, kicking, struggling against the unseen body behind her.

The pain was so sudden, so intense that everything went black. Her entire body convulsed in agony, and she was falling, falling, through the darkness of pain and emptiness, and she knew she was dying, and no one would help her, no one would save her. She flung out a hand as she landed, and as the void closed around her she managed to choke out a name.

McKinley stared down at her. She lay sprawled gracelessly on the dusty surface, half hidden by the underbrush. He stepped over her body and went to the car, careful not to touch anything. He could tell at a glance that Clancy had been dead at least a couple of hours, and there was no way Annie could have done it.

Not that he'd seriously considered her capable of it. But he took nothing for granted in this life. He'd once almost had his balls sliced off by a placid middle-aged nun. Annie Sutherland was, after all, Win's daughter. There was no telling what she was capable of. Whom she was working with.

He stepped away from the car, deliberately calm. He'd always liked Clancy. They'd shared a decent bottle of scotch on occasion, and more than one adventure. There weren't that many of his old friends left. None, with the exception of Martin. And even he might not be around for long.

He squatted down beside Annie's body. Her color was lousy, her breath was shallow and raspy, and he wondered why he'd stopped. A little more pressure, and he could have dumped her body in the car with Clancy's and taken off.

Hell, he didn't wonder why. He knew. She'd called his name, and he'd dropped her. She'd called his name, and he'd shown his first sign of weakness.

She was going to be the death of him. He knew it now with a bone-chilling certainty. He pushed her hair back from her face with a deliberately careless hand. A bruise was already forming at the base of her throat. She had the pale, soft skin that bruised easily. She would look in the mirror and know what he'd done to her.

He should have just let her go. But he didn't trust her. When he heard her sneaking out of the house, he'd gone after her. When he'd seen her head into the bushes, he'd been certain she'd be meeting a confederate.

Instead she was finding a dead body. Her second in less than six months. First there was Win, now Clancy.

There were going to be more.

Chapter Seven

She woke in darkness, in pain. Her neck felt stiff, paralyzed, and when she tried to turn it, streaks of agony shot through her body. She felt drunk, hungover in the murky night, and she closed her eyes again, trying to summon back the graceful twilight.

She could hear voices. Low, murmuring, from somewhere in the house. It took her a moment to remember where she was—the small, Englishy-cottage overlooking the L.A. canyons. She'd found . . . what was his name, Clancy? And someone had come up behind her and tried to kill her.

No, scratch that. If someone had tried to kill her, she'd be dead. And it wasn't just someone—in retrospect she knew exactly who'd come up behind her. James.

She could barely control a quiet whimper of pain as she sat up. She reached a trembling hand to her neck, pushing her hair away. It was raw, throbbing. What had the man done to her?

She moved to the door, then stopped. The voices were clearer now—James with the Texas in his voice, deceptively smooth and easy. And someone else, all quiet concern and stern disapproval. She knew that voice as well. Remembered it. Carew.

"I don't give a rat's ass what you think," James said affably. "If you didn't hit Clancy, then I want to know who did."

"I wouldn't be here now, I wouldn't have simply walked in, if I was in any way responsible for Clancy's death. He was in the business for years, McKinley, and he made a lot of enemies. You know that as well as I do."

"Pretty damned convenient for those enemies to choose today to snuff him."

"All right, so I don't believe in coincidences either. But I'm here, aren't I? I came as soon as I got your message. What do you want from me, Mack?"

Annie moved closer to the doorway, peering out into the hallway. They were at the bottom of the stairs, she guessed, their voices floating up toward her, and they were making no effort at discretion. Either Carew didn't know she was a witness. Or didn't care.

"I'll cut you a little deal, Carew. We both know I've tried to kill you twice. I was drunk then. I'm not drinking now, and you know that sober, there's no more dangerous man alive. If I put my mind to it, you're a dead man."

"You always did have delusions of grandeur," he said with a sniff.

"Give me a week. Let me find out who's left of Win's little sideline. Who helped him out. He didn't do it alone, even if you want to pretend he did. He was a smart man, but it was too complicated an operation for him to handle alone. I want to find out who was left. Who was with him when he turned. Who's going to try to keep it going."

"What if it's me?"

"Then you're a dead man anyway."

"It's not me." There was no missing the alarm in Carew's whiny voice.

"No," James said after a moment. "I don't believe it is. I want you to back off, Carew. Call off your little soldiers. You can't be sure who you can trust anyway. Which of them might be working for Win's replacement—"

"I trust them all!" he said sharply.

"Then you're a fool. You've still got a real problem, whether you want to admit it or not. Give me a week, and I'll take care of things. I don't make mistakes, and I don't leave loose ends."

"What do you call the woman upstairs?"

Silence, and Annie held her breath as she

waited for his answer. "A complication," he said finally. "One I can handle."

Annie moved down the first step, silent, even as the pain in her head threatened to explode. "I'm willing to deal," Carew said in a bitter voice. "You always knew that."

"Sure you are. When your back is against a wall and you know there's no way out. Well, this time, my friend, there's no way out."

She was halfway down the stairs by now, certain she was completely silent in the murky darkness. She could see their legs—they were standing in the living room of the cottage, and Carew was wearing beige linen trousers. James was wearing black.

"I must say I don't believe all this sudden nobility on your part, Mack. Is it money? You never were that interested in the kind of money you could have made in your line of work, or you wouldn't have been working for us."

"I don't need money."

"Then what the hell do you want from me?" Carew's voice rose to a frustrated shriek.

"Annie wants to know who killed her father. She's not going to rest until she finds out. And then she's going to want revenge."

Dead silence. "Jesus," Carew said softly. "So where's the problem? Handle it."

"No."

"I haven't seen any signs of you getting squeamish in your retirement, but I can always assign someone else. Assuming there's anyone left after you've gotten through with them," he added bitterly.

"You won't touch her. That's why I'm here. You're to keep your fucking goons away from her."

"Jesus, what happened to you, James? What the hell do you care what happens to Win's daughter?"

"I don't," he said flatly. "I just don't intend to let you clean up the mess you left behind. I'm not going to let you get off that easily."

"So?" Carew taunted him. "Then I can count on you taking care of her?"

"You can count on the fact that you better watch your back. I'm going to take her where she wants to go."

"It's your funeral, Mack. Are you really going to help her find out who did her father?"

"I'm going to help her find the answers she needs. Whether she likes it or not."

"Jesus," he said again. "What the hell are you getting yourself into, McKinley? What do you think you've got to gain by messing with all this?"

"Peace of mind maybe."

"It's a little too late for that, wouldn't you say?" The humor in Carew's voice was unpleasant. "You lost your chance for peace years ago."

"Maybe I'm curious. Maybe I just want to find the missing pieces of the puzzle."

"What missing pieces? It's straightforward enough, and you know it."

"I hate your guts, Carew, but I never thought you were stupid," James said in a level voice.

There was a pause. "Why don't you just ask me?"

"Because you don't have the answers any more than I do. You just want everything swept under the rug. That way you get to keep your job, and your power. But supposing I don't want things swept under a rug?"

"You made that more than clear."

"Tell you what, Carew. Let's have a little truce. I'll stop trying to kill you, and you can stop trying to kill me."

"Sounds reasonable," Carew said promptly.

"Not so fast. I don't believe you. I think you'll need a little incentive to back off."

"You're a dangerous man, McKinley. Don't you think self-preservation is a strong enough incentive?"

"You're smart, Carew, but you're arrogant. Look at it this way—if anything happens to me, or to Annie, then everything's going to blow up in your face. It'll make a stink so bad you won't ever get rid of it."

"It looks like that might happen anyway," he said in a sulky voice.

Annie moved down another step, crouching behind the railing, her hands tight with anger.

"It doesn't have to. I know they're regrouping. I can put a stop to it."

"How? And don't give me any crap about instincts—I don't believe in 'em."

"And that's why you made a lousy field operative."

"If he had a protégé, then the logical choice would be you."

"It would. But it wasn't." She could hear the icy drawl in his voice. "We're going to find out who he is, Carew. And I'll take care of him for you. I'll clean up the mess you're trying to ignore."

"You're crazy. Send Sutherland's daughter back to D.C. and we'll work something out. We can protect her, see that she's safe—"

"She stays with me. It's the only way I can keep her safe. Besides, I don't think she's going to give me any choice in the matter. Are you, Annie?" He pitched his voice toward the stairs, and Annie paused, clutching the banister.

"Jesus," Carew swore, whirling around. "You mean the bitch has been listening?"

Annie descended the stairs slowly, coming into the light. Carew was just as she remembered him, surprisingly attractive for such a narrow little soul. She'd always assumed he was a decade younger than James, but now she wasn't so sure. Beneath the carefully tanned skin and the contact-lensed eyes lurked an old, old man.

"You remember Carew, don't you, Annie?" James drawled with perfect civility.

Carew was a consummate actor. But then, she was learning they all were. All the men who'd surrounded her, lied to her, kept her safe in her cocooned little world of order and normalcy. "This has been a difficult time for you, Miss Sutherland," he said, moving swiftly forward and taking her limp hand in his. His grip was firm, warm, against her own icy skin. "I don't know what you think may have happened, but be assured that we'll do anything we can to help."

She pulled her hand away from him. It took all her effort not to plaster a polite smile on her face, not to murmur the appropriate, reassuring answer. She'd been trained as well, she thought. By a master.

"Can you think of any reason why I should believe you, Mr. Carew?" she said coolly. "Lies are more your style, aren't they?"

He didn't flinch, just kept that same con-

cerned expression on his face. As if he hadn't,
a few short moments ago, suggested that
James "handle" her. "I don't know what you
think you know, Miss Sutherland. I don't
know what James has told you, or what you've
figured out on your own, but chances are
whatever you're thinking, it's only part of the
truth. If lies have been told, they've been told
to protect you. Your father was involved in a
highly classified government project. The
fewer people who share information about
such projects, the safer it is all around."

"Not very safe for my father. Who killed
him?"

Carew didn't even flinch. "I'm sorry, Miss
Sutherland."

"And why? Why was he killed? Who placed
the order? Was it you?"

Carew shared a glance with McKinley.
James was leaning against the mantel, watching them in the gathering dusk, and Annie
hadn't the faintest idea what was going on behind his impassive gaze.

"You'll have to ask McKinley about that,"
Carew said with a faint sneer. "He's the man
with the answers."

The phrase rang in her head, like an unpleasant carillon, one that would sooner or
later make her crazy.

But Carew had already dismissed her.

"You've got your bargain, Mack," he said. "Hands off. I can't promise you forever. Let's say one week. And then it's out of my control. I answer to other people, you know."

"Yeah," he said. "And you lie to them as well."

Carew ignored the gibe, turning back to Annie. "I wish you'd come to me for help," he said in his soft, faintly plaintive voice. "Perhaps we could have found the answers you wanted without McKinley's theatrics."

"Sorry," she said, even as one hand absently kneaded her aching neck. "I trust James."

Carew's eyes were oddly colorless, almost reptilian in his handsome face. His gaze followed her hand to her neck, and there was only the slightest shift in his expression.

"I hope you don't live to regret it. But then again, that's exactly the problem. We can protect you from the men who killed your father. I'm not convinced that Mack can. Or will."

James said nothing. The shadows grew darker still in the room, but he made no move to turn on the lights. "I'm willing to take my chances," Annie said stubbornly.

Carew's smile was gentle and contemptuous. "I won't argue with you. It's your life. But if you happen to change your mind, don't hesitate to get in touch with me. That is, if

Mack lets you. I can offer you the best protection your government has to offer."

"It didn't do my father much good, did it?"

He blinked, then glanced back at James. "You know, I underestimated you, McKinley. You've managed to turn a reasonably intelligent human being into an idiot, just by crawling between her legs. I wouldn't have thought you were that good in bed."

Annie hadn't realized how fast James could move. Neither had Carew. In a matter of seconds James had him slammed up against the wall, one hand cradling Carew's throat, his long fingers wrapped halfway around it. It looked almost like a caress, and yet Annie had no doubt how very lethal that grip was. The sweat beading Carew's brow as he tried for a nonchalant smile told it all.

James's smile didn't help matters. It was cool and terrifying, and Annie could only be glad it wasn't directed at her. "You aren't really ready to die, are you, Carew?" he murmured softly.

"You wouldn't dare," Carew said in a tight voice. "You don't think I just walked in here without any backup. You know me well enough to know that I'd cover my ass. If I don't come out of here safe and sound, this place goes up like a tinderbox."

"And risk taking you along with it? I don't

think so." His fingers flexed, and Carew let out a small, strangled moan.

"Let me go, McKinley," he gasped. "Let me go or I'll—"

James released him so suddenly that Carew sagged against the wall, almost sliding to the floor. "Bastard," he muttered, rubbing his throat. He threw a sly glance over toward Annie, toward her own throat. "Watch your back, Miss Sutherland. And if you need help, I'll provide it. If he'll let you."

"You can leave now," James said with perfect courtesy. "We'll be in touch."

Annie found, to her absolute horror, that she wanted to giggle. James sounded like a prospective employer dismissing an unqualified applicant. She put her hand to her throat once more, leaving it there as some sort of unconscious protection, while Carew made a hasty retreat.

For a moment James stood in the darkness, his back to her. She started toward the light switch, suddenly unable to bear it anymore, but he caught her hand, her arm, whirling her around and stopping her before she could turn it on.

"Chances are he's got snipers trained at the windows," he said in a quiet, matter-of-fact voice. "If not Carew, then someone else. They've probably got infrared scopes as well, but we don't need to give them an illuminated target."

"Why would he want to have us killed? I thought he agreed to a truce."

"He's not the only one we have to worry about. As a matter of fact, I think he's the least of our problems. There are a lot of people who aren't too happy with the questions we've been asking. Don't believe him when he says he can protect you. Without me you're a dead woman, Annie. No ifs, ands, or buts."

"And with you?"

"You have a fighting chance."

It wasn't much of a consolation. She looked up at him. The darkness was so thick she could barely see his face, and for some reason she felt safer that way. "What's going to happen to us, James?" she whispered.

"We're probably going to die."

"You're very comforting," she said wryly. "Couldn't you lie a little bit? Just to make me feel better?"

She could feel the stillness in him. His hand was still on her arm, holding her, and she could feel a thousand unnamed emotions banked under his cool surface.

"I can lie," he said.

He released her, but she didn't move away. "Your friend . . ." she began. "Clancy."

"What about him?"

"He's dead."

"I know. I saw him."

"Is that what's going to happen to us?"

"If we're not lucky."

"What's luck got to do with it?"

"Everything."

"Did you . . . did you bring me back to the house?" She wasn't sure if she wanted to hear the answer. Except that she already knew it.

In the darkness he reached up and cradled her throat with one hand. He had big hands, strong, with long fingers that reached more than halfway around her neck. Long fingers that stroked her very gently, pinpointing the exact spot where the pain was the worst. "Yes," he said, his voice low and expressionless. "I knocked you out and brought you back here while you were unconscious."

"Why?"

He laughed. The sound was cool and faintly eerie in the enveloping darkness. "Why?" he echoed. "Because I didn't want to kill you."

She jerked herself away from him, and he let her go, making no effort to stop her. "Bastard," she snapped, thoroughly unnerved. "I suppose you think you're funny."

"A barrel of laughs, Annie," he murmured as she stalked from the room. "A barrel of laughs."

*　　*　　*

They were drawing back. His night vision was excellent, but even so, it was those instincts that Carew had derided that told him. The snipers were pulling back, and for the time being he and Annie were safe.

He had no particular illusions about how long it might last. He would take whatever advantage he could get, for as long as it lasted.

It was the only thing he could count on.

One thing was certain—he couldn't bring any more old friends into it. Clancy hadn't deserved to die that way—another soul on his conscience. Except that he had no conscience. And no more friends to risk, including Annie's ex-husband, Martin.

No, he'd be on his own from now on. Correction—they'd be on their own. He had Annie Sutherland, like a barnacle, like a clinging leech, like an albatross around his neck. One he didn't want to cut free.

He couldn't quite figure her out. She had no reason to trust him over Carew. She'd already known he'd half strangled her earlier that afternoon, and seeing him nearly do the same thing to Carew should have scared the hell out of her.

Instead it had only seemed to strengthen her resolve. She'd put herself in his hands completely.

He could hear Annie in the kitchen, making

a remarkable amount of noise. He looked down at his hands. The moon was rising over the canyon, sending a faint silvery light into the room, and he could see them quite clearly. An artist's hands.

An artist at dealing death.

They were going to have to deal more than death if he was going to keep Annie safe. He'd already made the decision, and much as he regretted it, he wasn't going back on it. He was keeping her with him.

His first problem was to figure out a way to keep her reasonably docile. Not that the word docile and Annie seemed to have much in common now that Win was dead. She was entirely rebellious, where once she had done everything her father had told her.

He needed to have her just where Win had. Blind, unquestioning obedience. He needed her to think what he wanted her to think, wear what he wanted her to wear, do what he wanted her to do. He needed her to have no mind or will of her own for the next week or so, while they went in search of the man who'd betrayed her father.

And in doing so, betrayed James himself.

There were any number of ways to bring Annie to heel. He could do it with threats, brute force, and intimidation. Easy and effective, but the victim was more likely to develop an unexpected streak of rebellion.

He could rely on friendship, shared memories and affection for her father. The weakest of all possible links, and one he didn't want to bet his, or her, life on.

He could use drugs, various forms of mind control, once he got access to them. He'd never had any particular liking for those recent innovations, but he was adept at using them.

Or he could use sex.

It was the least appealing of the possibilities. Sex was a two-edged sword—he was a man of phenomenal control, but that control had seemed more tenuous lately. Reckless. He wasn't certain of his ability to keep himself detached, even as he drew her in.

Unwanted, the memory of Mary Margaret Hanover came back to him. Mary Margaret in bed, on top of him, her long hair rippling down her back, her head thrown back in laughter, her full, perfect breasts bouncing up and down as she rode him.

And Mary Margaret, cool, slightly surprised, as his bullet entered her brain and she knew it was over.

He could fuck and kill if he had to, he knew that.

The danger was, he didn't know if he could fuck and kill Annie Sutherland.

"Do you want anything to eat?" He hadn't heard her return. She stood silhouetted in the living room door, the light from the kitchen illuminating her, and he turned slowly, knowing his face was in the shadows. There was no way she could guess what he was thinking. What he was considering.

What he might do to her.

"Yes," he said. "I'm hungry." And he started toward her.

Chapter Eight

She couldn't sleep. Annie lay in the old-fashioned bed underneath the eaves and watched the moonlight throw shadows across the polished wood floor, and she wondered if she'd ever sleep again.

Every time she closed her eyes, she saw Clancy's dead body slumped over the steering wheel.

She was living in a nightmare. One that had started the morning she'd found her father's body. Everything she'd believed in, everything she'd held sacred, had been turned upside down in the past six months. Her father was a stranger to her—the warm, slightly acerbic gentleman was becoming nothing more than a fairy tale, as unlikely as cowardly dragons or noble princes.

James was a lie as well. The quiet friend of her father's had vanished. She'd gone to him for help, expecting uncompromising strength and calm. Instead she'd found . . .

She didn't know what she'd found. She didn't know anything about the man she thought she'd known all her life. Except that he was dangerous.

But oddest, most disconcerting of all, was the fact that she didn't know herself anymore. Simple decisions were no longer simple. More and more often she'd found herself torn between what was obvious and right, and what her father would have wanted. And oddly enough, it was her father's wishes that seemed wrong.

If she'd had any sense at all, she would have gone into therapy, gone back to her muted colors and her muted life, and gotten on with things. Listened to Martin when he told her to leave things be. Leave James alone.

Instead she'd chucked it all and run off with the man who knew the answers. And she wasn't entirely sure she was ready to learn them.

She wondered where he was. There was no other bed in the tiny cottage, and the chintz sofa looked too small and too dainty for a man like McKinley. Maybe he could sleep standing up. Maybe he didn't need sleep at all.

Carew said she could change her mind, come to him for help. James said he was the only one who could keep her alive. And she had no idea who to believe, who to trust.

She glanced down at the thin Rolex her father had given her. Two forty-five in the morning, and just beyond the shadows lay a dead man. In the morning she might be dead as well.

When she awoke, the room was inky darkness. The moon had set, the wind had picked up, and there wasn't a sound beyond the rush of the leaves. She opened her eyes, and she knew she wasn't alone in the room.

"James?" she said, her voice almost unnaturally calm.

"Who else?" He sounded almost unbearably weary. "Time for us to get out of here." He loomed up over the bed, barely visible in the smothering darkness.

She had the odd notion he was going to touch her. And she didn't want him to. She scrambled off the bed, backing away from him. He made no move to follow her.

"How are we going to do that?" she asked. She was dressed in a light T-shirt and jeans, and the predawn air was chilly. She wasn't about to tell him so.

"Clancy."

Annie shuddered. "I'm not going in that car . . ."

"It's already been moved. Disappeared. Carew and his men can be very efficient when they need to be."

"What happened to him?"

She could see him shrug in the dim light, seemingly unconcerned. "His body won't be found. It won't matter—he had no family or friends outside the business. You learn to live a solitary life. No one will even notice his passing, much less mourn him."

There was an odd note in his voice, made even more noticeable by the darkness that surrounded them. "Is that what will happen with you?" she asked.

"Not if I'm lucky."

"What will happen if you're lucky?"

He moved closer, and there was no place for her to run. She'd already backed up against the wall, and she could only stand there, shoulders back, as he approached.

He stopped inches away, close enough that she could feel the tension that ran through his body. Close enough so that she could close her eyes and breathe in the strength of him, the sense of him, his power and his danger.

"If I'm lucky," he said, "I'll go out in a blaze of glory."

For a moment she didn't move. He didn't touch her, but then, he didn't need to. She felt touched, possessed, invaded, merely by his closeness. Somewhere she found her voice, and her defenses. "Are you sure you're thirty-nine?" she asked dryly. "You sound like an adolescent male."

The room was frozen in silence for a breathless moment. He moved then, putting his strong hands on her shoulders, and she flinched, unable to help herself, looking up at his shadowed face.

His long fingers splayed over her shoulders, his thumbs caressing her collar bone. "Be careful, Annie," he whispered, ducking his head closer to hers.

"I'm not afraid to offend you," she shot back, her voice wobbling just slightly.

"You don't offend me." The thumbs dipped lower, trailing across the tops of her breasts. "You . . ." He stopped, as if he was uncertain what to say. But James McKinley wasn't a man plagued by uncertainty, and she waited for him to finish.

"I . . . what?" she prompted.

He released her abruptly, and she fell back against the wall with a pronounced thud. "We'll talk about it when we're out of here," he said.

"And how are we getting out of here?"

"I told you, Clancy would have seen to it that we have a vehicle. I just have to hope we find it before the others do."

"The others? I thought Carew was going to leave us alone for the next week."

"Carew isn't our only worry, Annie. Besides, I don't trust anybody. He might do as he promised. Then again, he might not. I'm not about to risk your life on his word."

"What about your life?"

"That's expendable." He shoved a hand through his hair. "We've got one advantage. We're up against some impressive enemies, but they don't know the way Clancy's mind worked."

"And you do?"

"I've known him for a long time. I trusted him. I know the way he thinks."

There was no pain in James's voice. Nothing but simple common sense. Annie grabbed the duffel bag and slung it over her shoulder, prepared to follow him. "Don't you care?"

He was already out the door, and he didn't pause, tossing the question back at her. "About what?"

"About Clancy being dead. You were friends. Close friends, it sounds like. Doesn't it bother you?"

He started down the narrow stairs, and she almost missed his reply. "I'm used to it."

He didn't need to tell her to be quiet, to do as he said. She'd already learned the drill. She melted into the shadows behind him, moving almost as noiselessly as he did. The sky was just beginning to turn a paler blue, off to the east, and she glanced down at the luminous dial on her watch. Just a little before five.

"Is anyone here?" she whispered.

"Two, maybe three operatives," James said. "Probably Carew's men, and that's bad enough. If the one who did Clancy is out there too, we're in trouble."

"You mean we weren't before?" she asked wryly.

Once more he froze, looking down at her. "You pick a hell of a time to develop a sense of humor." He didn't give her time to respond. "Stay put."

A moment later he vanished into the darkness, leaving her alone in the kitchen.

She took a deep breath, then realized absently that her palms were sweating, her heart was pounding, and her breath was ragged. She was frightened.

It shouldn't have surprised her. As she stood motionless in the empty house, she knew what she was listening for. The sound of gunshots. The sound of James's death.

It all seemed so unreal. She wanted to cross the room, flick on the lights, turn on a radio. She wanted noise, she wanted normalcy. This had to be a bad dream.

But unbidden, the memory of Clancy's body

came back to her. And she knew it was no dream.

She slid down to the tile floor, pulling her knees up to her chest and wrapping her arms around her legs. She was cold, she was frightened, and if she had any sense at all she would have never embarked on this fool's errand, where nothing was as it seemed. She would die, alone in this kitchen, and there'd be no one to mourn her. She put her head down on her knees, closing her eyes, concentrating. The dawn was perfectly still.

"Annie?"

She almost screamed, but he slapped his hand over her mouth so quickly that her head slammed against the wall. She couldn't see him in the darkness, but she knew him— the sound of his voice and the feel of him. He gauged her acceptance perfectly, dropping his hand when she no longer needed to scream.

"You startled me," she whispered. "I didn't hear you come back."

"You weren't supposed to," James said.

"Is there anyone out there?"

"Not now," he said calmly. "I think I know where Clancy would have left a car for us. There's an old shed halfway down the hillside that looks about his style. Let's go."

She scrambled to her feet, once again loath

to let him touch her. She didn't know why she thought he'd want to. But it was there, between them. And she knew he would touch her. Sooner or later.

There was a faint, unexpected scent on the morning air. Metallic, sulfurous, caught on the drifting breeze. She tried to ignore it as she followed James down an overgrown path in the dawning light, tried not to test the air for other, more desperate odors.

"James," she said, her voice little more than a whisper. She half hoped he wouldn't hear her, but he was aware of everything, and he stopped for a moment, though he didn't bother to turn around.

"What?"

The light was growing brighter now. Faint slivers of peach and rose spreading over the tangled hillside. If anyone was watching, they would be perfect targets, and yet James seemed momentarily unconcerned.

"Is there such a thing as a blood lily?"

He didn't answer. He just started walking again down the hillside. And she had no choice but to follow, fighting back the horrifying knowledge that threatened to overwhelm her.

She didn't need more than a pointed look from him when they reached the clearing by the old shed. She squatted down in the bushes, out of sight, preparing to wait for him.

He had his gun—she could see it as he paused outside the shed door. Odd, how she couldn't get used to the sight of weapons. Her father had always been contemptuous of handguns, and Annie had followed his beliefs. Now she was becoming very grateful for their existence.

He disappeared inside the shed, and she held her breath, listening. For the explosion of gunfire, for the sound of a struggle. For his voice telling her it was all right to follow him into the darkened interior.

Nothing.

The sun was just coming up behind her, and the eerie half-light was turning sharp and bright. She told herself she could count to one hundred, she told herself she'd do it in French just to make it slower. By the time she got to *quatre-vingt dix-huit* she knew she couldn't wait any longer, and she rose, half expecting a bullet to slam into the back of her head.

When she first stepped inside the shed she couldn't see him. The light was murky, with only faint slivers of sunlight fighting their way through the cracks in the old wood. He was standing in the corner, dark and silent, and she followed his gaze, half expecting a corpse.

"Hell and damnation," she said with a mix of horrified amusement and exasperation. "He left us a motorcycle."

"Not just any motorcycle." James's voice was odd, muffled, distant. "It's a Vincent Black Shadow. Probably 1954 or thereabouts."

"So he left us an old motorcycle," Annie said. "Do you think it will still run?"

"It'll run," James said. He tossed a helmet at her, and she caught it, watching as he pulled his own on. With his dark clothes and his height he looked absurdly dangerous.

"I wouldn't have thought you'd be the type to worry about helmets," she said, pulling her own on.

"I'm not. They make us harder to recognize." He climbed onto the motorcycle with the studied grace of someone who knew exactly what he was doing.

"I take it you know how to ride one of these things?"

"Yes."

"Did Clancy know that about you?"

"Yes."

"I assume this motorcycle has some sentimental value—"

"Get the fuck on the back of the bike,

Annie, and stop talking," he said in a harsh voice. "We need to get out of here, not waste time discussing hobbies."

She did her best to appear nonchalant as she came up to him. She knew what she had to do—there was an obvious place for her directly behind him on the wide seat. All she had to do was throw her leg over and climb on. She didn't move.

"What are you waiting for?"

"I've never ridden a motorcycle before," she admitted, looking at the huge black machine with distrust.

"I should have known. Win kept you in a bell jar, didn't he? His perfect dancing princess, without a thought or a care of her own. Throw your goddamned leg over the bike and hold on."

"But—" She didn't have time for any more arguments. He caught her arm and yanked her, and she could either mount it or knock it, and them, over. She settled on the back gingerly.

"Put your arms around my waist," he growled.

She didn't want to do that either. "Isn't there someplace I can hold on . . . ?" Her voice trailed off in a squeak as he grabbed her wrists and hauled her against him. Her breasts were squashed against his broad back, but she had enough sense not to release him.

The engine roared to life. It didn't sound like a forty-year-old machine—it sounded new and elegant. A moment later they were speeding out into the dazzling sunlight, and all she could do was shut her eyes and try to keep from screaming.

She lost track of time. She was afraid to open her eyes, afraid to open her mind. As they sailed down the hill, she could still feel those eyes watching her. Still feel the target at the back of her neck.

She could feel his heart beat through their bodies. Two thin T-shirts separated them, and she could feel his heat, his bones, his breath, and his pulse as he gunned the motor and took them farther and farther away from that lovely little cottage with the stench of death all around it.

She couldn't rest her face against his back with the helmet in the way, a mixed blessing. All she could do was trust him, completely. She'd made her choice, and now she'd stick with it.

It no longer mattered where they were going. She'd thrown in her lot with him. She tightened her hands around his waist and hung on, shutting off her mind.

*   *   *

The Vincent purred beneath him, a magnificent machine from a better age. He glanced down at it in the bright sunlight. Probably as old as he was, perhaps older. A fitting farewell present from his old friend Clancy.

He told himself it didn't matter. Clancy had lived with the reality of death for as long as James had, knowing it could appear, unexpected, at any time. He'd come to their aid knowing it might mean his end, and he'd come willingly. Something else would have gotten to him sooner or later. He'd made too many enemies along the way, and Carew, or whatever asshole was behind all this, had too powerful a network.

James had learned not to feel guilt or regret. Not to mourn, not even to think about the past. He'd examined Clancy's body with detached calm, trying to pinpoint the trigger man's style, how long he'd been dead, etc., before he'd hauled Annie's ass back to the house.

He'd felt nothing during the long, sleepless hours of the night as he considered their options and how they'd get the hell away from there. When he relaxed he'd think about Clancy. About a time when they were young, full of passion and patriotism and justice.

And how they were old now. Empty inside. And Clancy was dead.

He must have known. They all had a sixth sense about it, the good ones. And the good ones were the only ones who made it for very long. When Clancy had stashed the Vincent Black Shadow in the shed, he would have sensed that it would be James who would come for it.

He was feeling too much, and it was dangerous. If someone had been hidden in the shed, waiting for him, he'd be a dead man now as well. And God knows what they would have done to Annie.

He wouldn't think about it. He could shut it off, neatly, surgically. Just keep moving forward, one step at a time. Get to the next stop, as fast as they could, and then deal with things.

She was holding on tightly, plastered to him. She was beginning to get that shell-shocked look around the eyes, as reality began to sink in, only to be summarily rejected. There was no way a woman like her could live with the reality of his life. Or her father's. If she had to face it, she'd be better off dead.

At this point he didn't plan on having her face it. He'd keep her with him, keep her safe, while he discovered his own answers.

And in the end, when he knew who had been working with Win, who'd been behind the setup, and his own eventual death sentence, then he'd finish things up. And Annie would be safe.

It was the least he could offer Win. The man he'd loved like a father.

She didn't know she had her arms wrapped tightly around an executioner. She didn't know he'd come back to the kitchen with the stench of death all around him. She didn't know, and she couldn't. Or it might drive her as mad as it was slowly driving him.

"I'm sorry, sir. McKinley and the woman got away."

"The hell you say! I sent some of our best people out there. You told me there was no way a car could have gone in or out, that the place was too isolated to walk out of."

"Yes, sir. Apparently I miscalculated."

"Apparently you did, son." The General leaned back, swirling a glass of single-malt scotch in one stubby-fingered hand. It would take a hell of a lot of scotch to take the edge off this disaster, and he was a man who watched his intake carefully. Too much liquor was a sign of weakness, and the General was a man without weakness.

He stared at the yuppie slime in front

of him. The new breed of bureaucrat—Ivy League–educated, politically correct, white wine–swilling faggots. He'd seen too damned many of them in the last few years, and if it was up to him he'd dump the lot in Iraq and let Hussein sort 'em out. They'd run crying home to mommy soon enough.

This one, though, was different, and the General had always known that. This one had the morals of a jackal, the brains and heart of a tiger. And no soul whatsoever. He had only to look into those empty, clever eyes and know that here was a man capable of absolutely anything.

It was a useful tool. And he was the General's tool, there was no doubting that. But like all tools, he had to be properly taken care of. Respected like the lethal weapon he was.

"So what do you intend to do about it?" the General asked calmly enough.

"I can take care of it. I just wonder how quickly we want to finish this."

"Damned quickly, son!" the general spat. "James McKinley has been a boil on my backside for months now, ever since he went rogue. He's a live wire, and this organization is too damned delicate to risk it. We've covered our tracks as well as we can, but we'd be fools to underestimate him, no matter how erratic he's gotten. If we want to get this up and running again, we're going to have to eliminate him before any more time passes. Before he can tell anyone else about what's been going on. He could get to us, son. He could bring us all tumbling down if we don't do something about him."

"Would you like me to handle it, sir?"

"Hell, yes, I'd like you to handle it! Haven't I already told you so a half dozen times?"

"And if Carew starts getting suspicious?"

"Handle him too. Hell, handle all of them. We can always blame terrorists. Or blame McKinley. Do you think the Sutherland girl knows about him?"

"I doubt it. She wouldn't have chosen to stay with him if she did, and Carew said it was definitely her choice."

"There's your way in, then. Drop a few key bits of information. Let her know what he does for a living, where he came from. That should scare the piss out of her."

"How do you suggest I do that without telling her everything? About the organization, about all of us?"

The General looked at him. There shouldn't have been any emotion, any regret in those soulless eyes, but there was. Even the best tool had its flaws, he thought absently. "If you can't see to it, son, I have plenty of people who can. It doesn't matter what she knows, what she guesses. She won't have a chance to pass it on. You tell her, get her away from McKinley. We'll take care of her, you take care of him. You do it fast. Is that clear?"

"As crystal, General."

"Then get on with it. Find 'em. Before they find us."

Chapter Nine

They were in the desert. She'd lost track of how long they'd been riding, or even where they'd been going. She simply closed her eyes and held on tight, with her arms around his waist, her knees tight to his thighs, letting her mind drift into some safe, quiet place where there was no blood or death. No moon rising over the barren landscape. Only bright, warming sunlight baking her back as they sped along the rough roads toward whatever destination James had in mind.

She knew they must have stopped, at least once, for a bathroom and for food, but she was only vaguely aware of it. Time blended together, and it seemed as if she'd been on the back of that sleek black motorcycle for years when the road beneath them became so rough that he had to throttle down, and she tightened her grip around him, afraid she'd be tossed off the back of the machine.

And not certain he'd come back for her if she was.

He finally stopped, turning off the engine, and she had no choice but to sit back and look around her, blinking in confusion. It looked like the trailer park from hell. There were a half dozen rundown mobile homes arranged in a haphazard fashion, surrounded by rusting automobiles and pickups. A broken toilet was set outside one of the worst-looking hovels, a mangy dog slunk through the shadows, glaring at them. The sun was already setting, and the chill that filled the air bit through Annie's thin T-shirt.

"We're here," James said, climbing off the bike.

Annie still didn't move. "Where's here?" It looked barren, bleak, and nightmarish, and much as she wanted to stop driving, she wasn't sure if this was where she wanted to stay.

He didn't answer, looking around him with a lack of curiosity that Annie found particularly chilling. He knew this place, knew it well. He'd chosen to come here, for whatever twisted reasons he might have.

He glanced back at her. "Are you coming with me or not?"

"Do I have any choice?"

"I doubt you'd be able to handle the Vincent. Right now you don't look like you could handle a tricycle. You need to get your land legs back."

He held out a hand for her, but she'd touched him enough that day. She'd had no choice, clinging to him on the motorcycle. She had a choice now.

She swung her leg off the motorcycle and slid to the ground, sinking to the hard-packed earth as her knees buckled beneath her.

He picked her up, of course, with all the impersonal care of a forklift operator, setting her on her feet and holding her arms for a moment until she steadied herself. Then he released her, obviously as loath for physical contact as she was.

The thought startled her, and she looked up at him, confused. He seemed almost unwilling to get close to her, and she wondered why. And she wondered why it bothered her.

"Why are you looking at me like that?" he demanded irritably.

She managed a weak shrug. "Just day-dreaming. Is there anyone else here?" She looked around him at the decrepit trailers.

"They keep to themselves. As we will." He started toward the most rundown of the structures. It was rusted, the small windows so streaked with grease and filth that she doubted any light would penetrate.

The light was fading fast. She was tired, she was hungry, and she needed a bathroom. She looked up at the place, wondering if it came equipped with indoor plumbing.

"This is where we're staying?" she asked, not moving.

"It's safe," he said grudgingly. "It might not be the Ritz, but it's better equipped for our needs. Unless you have a better idea."

She thought about it. "No," she said. "This is about the last place anyone would think of finding me." She followed him up the broken steps to the dented metal door.

That was when she noticed the locks. The trailer itself might be a disreputable pile of rusty metal, but the series of locks on the doors would have protected Fort Knox. And James held the keys.

She allowed herself a faint hope that the interior of the trailer might be similarly surprising, but the moment the smell of old beer, chili, and hot, stale air hit her, she knew that hope was in vain. She followed James into the darkened interior, but something made her stop for a moment, to look back over her shoulder at the place across the way.

There were no lights on in the afternoon

dusk, but she could see the movement behind the windows, and a chill ran over her.

"Someone's watching us," she said, skittering inside.

"Don't worry about it," he said. "Anybody out here is more concerned with covering their own ass than watching yours." He pushed the door shut behind her, closing them both into the heat and the darkness and the smell. She couldn't see him, but she could feel him, close, so close, and his arm slid past her face, and a sudden wild panic filled her.

Only to vanish as he switched on the light and then moved away.

She took a deep, calming breath. "It looks better in the darkness," she said. The one bare lightbulb hanging from the ceiling glared into the sparse interior. There was a kitchen at one end of the structure, a small living area in the center, and at the far end an alcove with a bed. One bed, with a bare mattress and a threadbare-looking blanket folded neatly at one end.

"All the comforts of home," she said wryly. "Is there a bathroom?"

"To your left. The plumbing even works."

"How do you know?"

"I know."

The bathroom was minuscule, complete with rusty shower stall, rickety toilet, and a tiny sink. She didn't care. She wanted that shower.

She heard voices as she was washing her hands. The water was rusty, brownish as well. She didn't care.

She opened the door slowly, carefully, expecting God knew what. Only to find James stretched out on the sagging sofa, a cold beer in one hand, staring at a tiny black-and-white TV set.

She wanted to hit him. She wanted to take her fists and beat against him, to pound his head against the wall and demand some answers. Once more he looked like a different man. Like a good old boy, stretched out, watching a football game. But he wasn't watching a football game, he was watching CNN. And this wasn't the kind of place that would have cable.

"There's food in the kitchen," he said. "And beer."

"I told you, I don't drink."

"I do."

There was nothing she could say to that. He was stretched out on the sofa, his long, black-clad body seemingly at ease as he stared at the flickering images on the television set, but she could see the handle of the gun tucked in his waistband.

There was bottled water, cans of chili and

beef stew and soup, ramen noodles and tuna fish. She settled for tomato soup and crackers, not bothering to offer James any.

There was no other place to sit but the old sofa. She perched next to him, as far away as she could manage, concentrating on the television as well.

"Anything interesting?" She made a belated attempt at sociability.

"Brush fires in California," he said casually. "They think it started up in one of the canyons. Some old cottage caught on fire, and it spread from there."

She stopped eating. "Did you do it?"

"Do what?"

"Start the fire."

"No. I think we can probably thank Carew for that. Covering up his mistakes."

"What mistake did he make?"

"Letting us leave," James said, draining his beer. "I'm going out. You stay put. Don't answer the door, don't answer the telephone."

"There's a telephone?" she asked in frank disbelief.

"A cellular phone in the bedroom."

"What the hell is this place?" she asked again. "Where are we?"

"A bolt hole," he said. "That's all you need to know. We're safe for the next couple of days."

"You said that when we got to the cottage."

"Yeah, but the only other person who knows about this place is Clancy. And he's dead."

There was absolutely no emotion in his voice or face. Either he simply didn't care, or he was a phenomenal liar. She wasn't sure which she'd find more reassuring.

"Where are you going?" She hoped her voice didn't sound quite as forlorn as she felt. She didn't want to be left alone in this strange place. He was little comfort, but he was better than nothing.

"Shopping."

"For what?"

"Tequila. Food. Information."

"All right," she said, knowing he wasn't asking permission. "I think I'll take a shower and go to bed. Where do you want me to sleep?"

She must have imagined the undercurrent that shot between them. "You can use the bed again," he drawled. "I don't need much sleep."

"I don't suppose this place comes equipped with clothes?"

"You can wear some of mine. You'll find them in the drawers under the bed."

"You own this place?"

Once more he wouldn't answer. "Lock the doors behind me," he said. Slamming his empty beer can down on the cheap side table, he pushed off the couch, and a moment later he was gone.

She leaned back, staring sightlessly at the television set while she listened to the motorcycle start up with a quiet roar, then fade away in the distance. And she wondered whether he'd come back for her.

The black-and-white flames ate into the hillsides surrounding Los Angeles, and she blinked at the vision. It should have looked less threatening in black-and-white. Instead it looked even more hellacious.

"So far there have been only the six casualties, but officials are fearing the death toll may rise substantially. The four bodies at the house in the hills outside Los Angeles have yet to be identified, but the coroner expects the information to be forthcoming."

Four bodies. They didn't say which house in the hills, but it didn't matter. She knew which house. She knew who one of those bodies was. Clancy, with the wry smile and the Vincent motorcycle. The man James stubbornly refused to mourn.

But who were the other three? And how had they died?

Maybe she didn't want to know that either. She clicked off the television set and headed toward the shower. The water was hot, the rusty brown turned almost clear by the time she was finished, and she wrapped herself in a threadbare towel before heading into the tiny bedroom alcove.

The clothes in the drawers beneath the bed were serviceable. She pulled on a big T-shirt and pair of running shorts and climbed up onto the bed. Trying to ignore the boxes of ammunition that lay beneath the neatly folded underwear.

The bed was as hard and lumpy as it looked, the blanket thin and scratchy. She didn't care. She didn't care that her body ached from the endless ride over bumpy roads. She didn't mind that her hair was wet and tangled as she lay on the pillow. She didn't even care that there were four dead bodies in the house they'd left just that morning.

All she cared about was that she was alone. And she had no guarantee whatsoever that James would be coming back.

She switched off the light, lying in the darkness. The moon had risen, sending a faint glow through the grease-stained windows. The rest of the decrepit little trailer was surprisingly clean for all its rust and decay, and she realized the windows were obscured for a reason.

There was a reason for everything James did, and the notion was far from reassuring. She still didn't know who or what he was.

But she knew, despite her misgivings, that he'd come back for her. And he'd keep her safe. No one would get to her, no one would hurt her. James would see to that.

And she closed her eyes, sinking into an exhausted sleep.

Carew despised General Donald with his entire soul, and he was counting the days when he wouldn't have to deal with him ever again. During the years he'd been working under Win Sutherland, following his mentor's orders, he'd run afoul of the military, in particular General Donald. The man had done everything he could to interfere with the smooth running of the organization, and then, when Sutherland had been taken out, he'd been trying to horn in ever since.

Well, let him, Carew thought pettishly. If they could just clear up the few ugly loose ends, then the entire mess could be neatly covered up. There was little use for people like McKinley nowadays. Once things were cleaned up, Carew intended to devote his career to budgetary matters. Cloak-and-dagger stuff wasn't nearly as exciting as money.

And people like General Donald never bothered with finances, except to ask for more. Carew had every intention of being in the position to tell him no.

"What the hell have you done with McKinley and the girl?" The General didn't even wait until he could take a seat in the walnut-lined office. "I would have thought you could handle a simple matter like that. They can't have just disappeared off the face of the earth."

"I don't know," said Carew.

"And who the hell botched the fire? We're not supposed to have civilian casualties. It gets the press too excited, and it's even worse when they're children. You'd think no child ever died in war," he said with a dismissive wave of his hand. "I've always said this operation should be under military jurisdiction. But does anyone listen?"

"I don't know that either, General."

"Well, son, you don't know a hell of a lot, do you?" The General rose, coming to loom over Carew.

Carew didn't flinch. He was used to men like the General. Men who tried to use their size, their bluster, to intimidate. Carew wasn't a man who was intimidated easily. He was a survivor. He had to be to have lasted this long, to have risen so far. He wasn't about to let a petty bully like the General stop his forward advancement. "No, sir," he said politely, looking up at his nemesis.

"You want a smoke?" the General barked,

and Carew knew it was some stupid test of manhood. One he'd fail.

"No, thank you, sir. I don't smoke."

The General muttered something beneath his breath, glaring at him. "What do your people say? You talked to any of them? Some of them used to work with Sutherland, and with McKinley. They must have some idea where they could have gone. What about Hanover? Clancy? Paulsen?"

"Hanover and Clancy are dead," Carew said carefully. "McKinley did Hanover when she came for him in Mexico. And I don't know who did Clancy. It wasn't us, and I doubt it was James. They went way back."

"I doubt McKinley's ever troubled by sentimental attachments," the General snapped. "What about Paulsen?"

"If he knows, he's not telling."

"Jesus fucking Christ," the General exploded. "And you let him get away with that shit? I could get it out of him in five minutes flat."

"I don't think he knows."

"Thinking's not good enough, Carew. I want that information. I want McKinley, and I want Sutherland's daughter. I want them taken care of, do you hear me?"

Carew glanced up. He almost wished he did smoke—he would have blown some in the

General's fat red face. "Why?" he asked calmly.

"They're a danger. You know that as well as I do. McKinley should have been neutralized months ago. But you blew it, and now Sutherland's daughter is caught up in it as well. You find where the hell they are, and I'll take care of it from there. We can't afford any more fuck-ups, Carew. Not if you want to keep your job. Not if we want to keep the organization going. You hear me, son?"

Carew rose. He'd hated his own father with an adolescent passion that had rejoiced in the bastard's death in a car accident. It was nothing compared to how much he hated the General.

"I'll talk to Paulsen," he said in a deceptively mild voice. "I'll handle it."

"See that you do, boy. Because if you can't, I can."

And as Carew left, he once more mourned the death of Mary Margaret Hanover. If McKinley hadn't gotten to her, she could have cut the General's throat for him. The bittersweet notion gave him his first smile in days.

She wasn't alone. The bed was hard, wide, and when she opened her eyes in the murky light she could see James stretched out beside her, seemingly sound asleep.

She started to sit up, but his hand shot out, clamping around her wrist. "Go back to sleep," he said, his mouth barely moving, his eyes still shut.

"You said you were going to sleep on the sofa."

"I said I didn't sleep much. I didn't say where I was going to sleep."

She yanked her arm, but his fingers might have been a handcuff. She was tired, she was angry, and she was frightened. Without thinking she slammed her other hand against his chest.

His response was so fast it was terrifying. In less than a second she was flat on her back, and his hand was cradling her neck. It was no lover's caress. His thumb pressed up underneath her jawline, and the pain was breathtaking. "Don't," he said in a mere breath of a voice.

As a warning it was completely effective. She couldn't move, couldn't nod her head or even speak. She simply looked up at him out of wide eyes, waiting for him to increase the pressure. To kill her. Or release her.

She really didn't know which it was going to be. She suspected he didn't either, at least for the moment.

And then he dropped his hand, rolling onto

his back, taking deep gulps of air, as if he'd been running very fast.

It took all her fierce will not to try to bolt once more. He wouldn't let her get far, she knew it, and this time he might kill her. She lay back beside him, her own breathing equally harsh, and waited.

"Don't underestimate me," he said finally, when his breathing had slowed to a reasonable rate. "I act on instinct, and that can be very dangerous."

"What happened to those people?"

"What people?"

"There were four bodies found at the cottage. I figure one was Clancy. Who were the other three?"

He didn't hesitate. "I don't know."

She was willing to believe that much. "What happened to them?"

"I killed them."

The words, three simple ones, hung in the air. She waited for horror and panic to fill her. Nothing happened, and she understood why.

"I think I knew that," she said quietly.

"No one ever said you weren't bright enough. Aren't you going to ask me why?"

"I assume they were trying to kill us."

She darted a quick glance at him, and despite his expressionless face she could see a faint quirk of bleak amusement. "Logical as well," he said. "Any other questions?"

He was being surprisingly forthcoming, and she racked her brain for the right question. The one that came out surprised her.

"How old was your wife when she died?"

"My wife?"

"When you started to work for my father," she said patiently. "Your wife and child had died in a car accident, and you left east Texas and . . ." Her words trailed off. "Why don't you sound the same? Where's your accent?"

"Wouldn't I have lost it after all these years?"

"You wouldn't have lost it in a matter of days," she said. "You always had a faint Texas accent."

"Did I? I've never lived in Texas in my life."

She absorbed that as she would a blow. "And your family?" she persisted.

"You mean that romantic fantasy your father concocted? How's your math, Annie? I joined your father twenty years ago. I'm thirty-nine. Do you think I had a wife and a baby?"

"No."

"Bingo."

"Then where did my father find you? How did he recruit you for his mysterious organization?"

"Let's just say he offered me a job when I

was in need of one," he said evenly, pushing back against the limp pillows. He was watching her closely, and she wanted to move away from him. But she'd seen how fast he could move, and she didn't dare. "You don't need any more details."

"In other words, you aren't going to give me any more details," she murmured. "Are you gay?"

She'd finally managed to startle him, and he smiled. It wasn't a reassuring expression. "Would it make you feel better if I was?"

For a moment she didn't respond. And then she shrugged. "It wouldn't make any difference. What you are is sexless. A machine, a cipher, a good little soldier. Your sexual preference, even if you had one, doesn't have anything to do with me."

"Yes, it does," he said.

The words hung in the air, heavy, weighted, profoundly sexual. She recognized it with a tremor that reached deep inside, and she no longer cared if he hurt her, killed her. She had to get away from him. From the threat of him.

She rolled off the bed and backed away from it. He made no attempt to come after her—simply lay there watching her out of hooded eyes.

"There's no place to run to, Annie," he said. "You're only safe with me, and you know it."

"Am I safe with you?" It sounded too damned plaintive, but there was no way she could make her voice stronger.

"As safe as you can be."

"And how safe is that?"

He looked at her, and she knew he would tell her the truth whether she really wanted to hear it or not.

"Not safe at all," he said.

And she nodded, believing him.

Chapter Ten

She'd forgotten. It shouldn't have surprised him—it was a lifetime ago, and she was probably happier pretending it had never happened.

He knew the feeling. For the past few years he'd put it out of his mind as well, keeping his distance from her so he wouldn't be tempted again. Win had known, of course. It had probably given him great amusement. He'd mentioned it only once, just enough to twist the knife.

He could hear her moving around in the trailer. The place was sturdy enough—the crummy-looking walls were reinforced with sheets of a bulletproof alloy that had cost a small fortune. It was also completely safe. The cellular telephone was hooked up through an elaborate relay that made him impossible to track. No one would find them—he could take his time figuring out what to do with her. And whether he was going to have to face his past.

He could start small. He could let himself remember what he'd worked so hard to forget. That night, years ago, that he spent with Annie Sutherland. The last time he'd been fool enough to let down his guard.

He'd never known for sure whether Win had set him up. Win was so firmly possessive of his only child—and his protégés, for that matter—that James couldn't believe he would have thrown them together, risking an alliance that might have shut him out.

But Win was also controlling enough that it seemed unlikely it simply could have happened by accident. As it was, James would never know. He'd always avoided discussing Annie with her father, and now it was too late. Win was dead.

She had been twenty-one. An oddly, achingly innocent twenty-one, when his life had been rank with the smell of death and decay. Her innocence had nothing to do with whether she'd had lovers or not. It was deep in her bones, born there, and Win had done his best to foster it. Perhaps he'd wanted to protect his only child. But he'd also enjoyed the irony of innocence born out of corruption.

She was home from college that Thanksgiving weekend, and Win had wanted all his young protégés to come to dinner. Mary Margaret had been invited, not much older than

Annie and already a seasoned killer. Martin and Clancy, Billy Arnett and his young wife, and a couple of others whose names he couldn't even remember. They were dead now, most of them.

Annie had insisted on cooking. James had accepted that information with mixed feelings—Annie Sutherland had grown up with a cook and a housekeeper, and if she even knew how to scramble an egg it was news to him.

He arrived mid-morning with papers for Win, only to find the house deserted, Annie in the kitchen, tears pouring down her face.

His first instinct had been panic. Someone had finally gotten to Win, and James hadn't been around to protect him.

And then he'd seen the turkey.

"It's frozen!" she'd wailed.

"They usually are."

"But, James, I've had it sitting in the fridge for days. I think I've got frostbite from trying to pull that disgusting stuff out of it, and even boiling water won't loosen it. And the oven's too small to hold everything, and I tried to call Win's caterer, but he's not answering, and I don't know what to do!" She had tears in her eyes, real tears, and he stared down at her, momentarily bemused.

He'd known Annie Sutherland since she was seven years old and he was nineteen. He'd come to this country, to Win, a raw bundle of rage and nerves, and it was only the presence of a child that somehow managed to work its way past his fury and touch some long-lost core of humanity.

He'd always felt grateful to her for that. But looking down at her then, in tears over her stupid turkey, he realized she was no longer a child. And gratitude had nothing to do with what he was feeling.

It hit him, fast and hard, so unexpected that he had no defenses. He wanted to pull her into his arms, dry her tears, and then kiss that pale, trembling mouth. He wanted to shove the damned frozen turkey on the floor, set her down on the table, and lift up her long skirts. He wanted to put his mouth on her, and see what she did.

He didn't touch her. "You got another apron?" he said with his perfect Texas drawl, glancing around him.

Her eyes widened, the tears vanishing. "James, do you know how to cook?"

"No Texas mother would let her son out into the world without knowing how to fend for himself," he replied, stripping off the charcoal gray suit that was part of his bureaucratic camouflage. In fact, his mother had taught him to cook, all right, but she'd never left

Northern Ireland before a sniper's bullet ended her life at thirty-seven.

"Oh, thank God," she breathed. "You're a lifesaver."

That was the one thing he wasn't. He was a lifetaker, a professional, a fact he accepted without bitterness or rancor. Until he looked into her ingenuous eyes.

He rolled up his sleeves, stripped off his tie, and headed for the turkey. It was a massive creature, still half frozen, and the boiling water she'd poured into the cavity had solidified. "Is the oven on?"

"I turned it off," she admitted.

"Take the top rack out. Then turn it to four hundred." He dumped the frozen bird in the black-speckled roasting pan.

"You can't cook it like that," she protested. "It's not stuffed."

"It will be. We'll start it out, and in a half hour things should be warm enough to finish prepping it."

"And we won't all die of salmonella poisoning?" she asked suspiciously.

"There are worse ways to go," he murmured, shoving the turkey in the fancy steel oven. "What else are we having?"

"I don't suppose you know how to make pies?" she asked in a plaintive voice.

He just looked at her. She had flour on her

nose—he'd missed that before. Her blond hair was screwed up in some sort of knot on the top of her head, but it was falling down. She was wearing a frilly apron with a turkey on it, and she looked so damned normal, surrounded by kitchen chaos, that he wanted . . . he wanted . . .

He wasn't sure what he wanted. It was all tied up with sex and violence, and he was going to indulge in neither. "What's the problem with the pies?" he asked wearily.

It was an odd day, almost surreal. A light snow was falling outside the multipaned windows, but inside the spacious kitchen of Win Sutherland's Georgetown house everything was cozy and warm. The air was rich with the smell of roasting turkey and baking pies, and what James couldn't remember from his mother they improvised with cookbooks and with laughter. They created a feast—slightly scorched, but a feast nonetheless. A normal, happy celebration of an American holiday. And for those few hours James was content to do something very dangerous. To pretend.

There was no cramped flat in Belfast with too many children and never enough money. There were no snipers, no bombings, no jobs so filthy that they slowly, deliberately ate at his soul, draining it, crushing it, so that he was left without it. An empty shell of a man.

She had a crush on him. She'd developed it a little more than a year ago, and he'd done his best to avoid her ever since. Win had informed him of it with great amusement, but James hadn't been amused. Annie was too young, too unsullied despite her family connections. He wasn't going to contaminate her even enough to dream.

But now he was here, Win was nowhere to be seen, and surrounded by the homey normalcy of it all, James found his defenses were vanishing. When she smiled up at him, that damnable light in her blue eyes, he wanted to see himself with that same light.

Instead, it was all he could do not to take her by the arms, slam her up against the wall, and say "Look, Annie, I'm not what you think I am."

But he couldn't. The truth would hurt her, far more than it would him. The truth would endanger her. And shatter her trust in her father.

No, he wasn't going to say a word. He was going to suffer through her gently flirtatious behavior; he was even going to flirt, ever so carefully, back. Because he knew it would hurt him even more, and he wanted to hurt himself.

"It's perfect," she breathed, looking at the table. It was set with heavy sterling and Waterford crystal, Limoges and damask. And he thought of his ancestors, starving, while rich landowners drank fine French wines from the crystal his countrymen made with their sweat and blood, and the anger came back to him, so that he was seventeen again, and crazy with idealism and what he thought was the truth.

He said nothing, glancing out at the snowy afternoon. The stuff was coming down harder now, plastering against the windows, and he realized it had been awhile since he'd seen any sign of traffic on the normally busy streets. They were alone in the house, he and Annie Sutherland. Shut away from reality, from the constant mortal dangers of his everyday life. They were alone, and he wanted her.

The darkness was as subtle as a clap of thunder, hammering down around them. "The power must have gone off," Annie said in a small, slightly nervous voice. Moving closer to him in the shadowy dining room.

He found he had automatically steeled himself for an attack. He took a deep breath, relaxing, and found he was breathing in the scent of her perfume as well as the rich smells of holiday cooking.

"I've got a battery-operated stereo in my bedroom. Maybe we can see what's going on in the world outside," she said.

"Maybe we don't want to know."

He didn't have to see her face to know her expression. Faintly quizzical, but accepting. "Ignorance is seldom bliss," she said with just a trace of wryness.

"I wouldn't be too sure of that." He moved away from her, needing to, leaning over and lighting the silver candelabra with his lighter, filling the room with a warm glow.

She looked ethereal in the candlelight. Dangerously so. And she hadn't the faintest idea what she was doing to him, how she was fighting her way past decades of defenses, like acid eating through steel.

She must have felt something. She didn't move, but she looked up at him, and there was a smoky yearning in her eyes. One he was determined to ignore. He turned his back to her deliberately, walking over to stare out the window into the snowy street.

"I'll go get the radio," she said, and if he hadn't been so attuned to her he wouldn't have heard the quiet resignation in her voice.

It wasn't until he heard a crash that he realized she hadn't taken a candle with her. He didn't allow himself time to think, to consider. He was halfway up the stairs, his gun drawn, when he found her huddled in the darkness.

He hadn't brought any form of light either, and it was inky black. He knelt down beside her, tucking the unseen gun behind his back.

"What happened?" He didn't touch her. He had the perfect excuse, but he didn't dare. He knew he wouldn't stop.

"Just clumsy," she said. "I thought I knew this old house well enough to find my way in the dark, but I guess I was wrong." She came to her feet, and he started to back away from her, listening, trying to sense if she was hurt.

But she reached out for him, touching him in the dark. Her hand on his arm, and she smelled like flowers and innocence. She smelled like every dream of adolescent sex he'd never been able to indulge in. And he wanted to.

"You mind coming with me?" she asked. "This place makes me a little nervous in the dark."

He wanted to pull away. He knew it wasn't a come-on. Or if it was, she didn't know what she was asking for. "You think there are bogey men in here?" he said lightly.

"I doubt it. Father's got enough security equipment to guard Fort Knox."

"It wouldn't work with the power out."

"You trying to make me feel better, James? If you are, it's failing. Come on." She released him, but he could still feel the grasp of her hand on his arm. The imprint of each long, elegant finger. And she'd barely touched him.

He went with her. Past the second floor,

where Win slept in baronial splendor. Up the narrow stairs to the third floor, to a room he'd never seen.

He'd forgotten she slept up there. Away from Win's soundproofed rooms and interesting habits. She even had her own back stairs down to the kitchen, he remembered vaguely. But he'd deliberately kept away from the third floor since she reached puberty.

There was only a fitful light coming from the snow-crusted window at the end of the third-floor hallway. He was closer to her than he wanted to be, and he cursed himself for not bringing a candle, a flashlight, anything to break the cocoon of erotic gloom that hovered around them.

He stopped right inside her door, leaning against it as he listened to her move around in the darkness. The scents that were uniquely Annie were stronger than ever. He could smell her perfume, the shampoo and water from the shower, even the toothpaste she used. He could smell the detergent on the sheets of her bed, could smell the leather from her shoes. He wondered where the bed was.

His eyes grew accustomed to the dark quite quickly. He'd always had extraordinary night vision—a boon in his line of work. He could see her silhouetted against the window, the shape of her, the rich, warm curves of her. And he could see the bed just behind her.

A big, high bed. Rumpled, unmade, the sheets tangled around what looked like a duvet.

He closed his eyes with a despairing sigh. It was the rumpled sheets that finished his resolve. If only the bed had been neatly made, with tight blankets you could bounce a quarter on, he could have resisted. But the gleaming white tangle of sheets needed to be wrapped around her naked body. And his. And he took the gun from his waistband, set it silently on the dresser by the door, and started toward her.

She must have felt him coming. She turned when he reached her, looking up at him, and there was no fear in her face. He touched her, cupping her cheek with his big hand, and she felt warm, fragile against him. He knew how fragile human flesh and bone could be.

She turned her face and pressed her mouth against his palm. "You taste of cinnamon," she whispered. And he wanted her to taste him.

She tilted her face up, brushing her mouth against his, a tentative gesture, as if she wasn't sure of her welcome. He slid his arm around her waist, pulling her soft, willowy body against him with careful deliberation, settling her against him, letting her feel how hard he was, and he set his open mouth against hers.

There was no hurry, no anger in the kiss. He simply held her against him as he slowly used his lips, his tongue, his teeth, to leave no part of her mouth untouched, unkissed. She was panting when he lifted his head, short, strangled little gasps, and she trembled in his arms. He told himself it wasn't fear, but he had felt fear too many times not to recognize it.

"Don't stop," she whispered, a mere breath of a sound, a plea.

He reached between them and touched her breast. She shivered—again that fear—but she moved against him anyway, and he accepted the truth. Her instincts told her he was death and danger even as she refused to admit it.

It would make sex powerful. To take her fear and use it in arousing her. It would make it too powerful for him to walk away from untouched. If he had any sense he'd step back, away from her.

But she was too close, too hot, too ready for him. She tasted too sweet. He began to unfasten the tiny buttons of the soft sweater she wore, when the lights glared into the room as the power came back on.

He jerked away from her as sanity came rushing back. It was a girl's room that surrounded him. The bed was a four-poster, complete with lacy canopy. She had a collection of dolls, for Christ's sake, and everything was pink.

"Thank God for the electric company," he said in a deliberately light voice.

She didn't move. Her eyes were wide, shadowed, and her mouth was damp and swollen. Her sweater was unbuttoned, and in the warm room he could see her nipples.

"Why?" she said very simply.

He'd already moved back, away from her, toward the door. He didn't want her to see the gun. As far as she knew, he'd have no reason to carry a weapon, certainly no reason to keep it with him right now. And he wasn't in any mood to explain. About anything.

"Why what?" he said warily. "Why did I kiss you?"

She shook her head. "I know why you kissed me. You wanted to. I'm not an idiot, James. You've wanted to kiss me for almost as long as I've wanted you to."

Something inside him snapped. His temper, his control. He leaned back against the dresser, retrieved the gun without her noticing. "Wrong, Annie. I don't want to kiss you. I want to fuck you. But I suspect your father would have something to say about that, and frankly, my friendship with him is more important than getting between your legs. As long and luscious as they are." He was using his Texas drawl to mocking perfection, and it eased some of his self-loathing. This was James McKinley. Good ole boy. It wasn't the man who'd just kissed Annie Sutherland in her bedroom.

"I see," she said in a subdued voice.

"Besides, I would have hated like hell to wake up and found I'd slept in a pink bedroom."

"I could paint it." The words, soft and plaintive, haunted the room, haunted him.

He shook his head gently. "No, Annie."

She looked at him, and there was such pain and longing in her eyes that it almost broke him. Except that nothing broke him. Nothing touched him. Not an innocent child ready to throw herself at his feet, not his own voracious need for her. He was invulnerable.

And then she smiled. It wavered slightly, but it was close enough, even if he could still see that her mouth was damp from his. "Well, in that case, maybe we'd better get downstairs and see what's happening with the dinner. It's just as well. I hate to paint."

He let her go ahead of him. He didn't want her to glimpse the gun. By the time they reached the bottom flight of stairs, the lights had dimmed once more, and he could hear the icy pellets pounding against the house.

"I hope Win's all right," she said in a subdued voice. "He was supposed to fly in from Los Angeles this morning, and he's already hours late."

Winston was flying in from Beirut, but Annie didn't need to know that. "I'm sure he'll call as soon as he can get to a phone."

"And what about the others?"

He wondered that himself. The ice storm might be enough to keep them away, but they would have called. There was something going on, and he'd been a fool not to realize it sooner. Too caught up with Annie Sutherland to wonder what the hell was going on.

Win had asked him to come by in the morning, and Win was nowhere around. Nothing happened without Sutherland being aware of it, behind it all, and James had no doubt he was exactly where he was supposed to be. It would have helped if he knew whether Annie was in any sort of danger, but it was typical of Win not to have told him. Not to have warned him. He'd know that if anyone could keep his daughter safe, James could. Whether he suspected danger or not.

Damn Win! he thought with sudden fury. His arrogance was so complete, his control so absolute, that he never considered there might be an alternative danger. An emotional danger between the two of them.

"The others will show up sooner or later," he said in a cool voice, as the dimming lights blinked off entirely. "It's an electric oven, isn't it?"

"Yes. Electric heat as well. Don't you think the power will come on again? It was only out for about ten minutes before." She sounded completely unconcerned. Maybe she thought she was safe from him. Maybe she thought he wasn't safe from her.

"The power will come back on. It's just a question of how long it will take. That's freezing rain out there, and when that happens the electric company gets depressed. Add the holiday into that equation, and we might be looking at a long stretch without power."

The dim glow of the candlelight filtered from the dining room. "And we forgot the radio."

"I don't think we ought to go back upstairs for it," he said in a deliberately soft voice.

"You're probably right." She didn't sound convinced.

"Why don't you take the candles and go into the library?" he suggested. "I'll find us something hot to drink and see about building a fire in the fireplace. It's already feeling chilly in here."

"That's your Texas panhandle blood," she said. "You aren't used to rough winters."

He could remember the bitter cold of an Irish January in that unheated flat. "Yeah," he drawled. "This is too tough for a country boy like me."

He took his time, telling himself he needed to keep his distance, needed to remember who and what he was. Win trusted him, for God's sake. Wherever he and the others were, they were counting on him to keep Win's daughter safe. Not humping her brains out.

He found the sherry and poured them both a glass. He hated sherry—it was too thick and sweet, and he drank it deliberately. He usually drank bourbon to go with his Texas persona, though he would have preferred the good Irish. But right now he didn't dare drink anything stronger than fortified wine. He was holding on to his sense by a thread. It wouldn't take that much for the thread to snap.

He found the answer to one of his first questions when he tried to make a few phone calls. The phone line was dead. He had no idea whether it was the ice storm or human interference, but he could only assume the latter if he wanted to keep them safe. He'd lied to her when he told her the security measures were off with the power. Win had the kind of backup that allowed for the vagaries of Washington weather, and it would still take a heavily armed combat unit to get inside.

And then they'd have to deal with him.

But Annie wouldn't understand why her father would have that kind of security. And he wasn't going to be the one to explain to her.

Any more than he was going to explain the presence of the gun he carried. He was far more lethal with his bare hands, but with everything so uncertain he needed every advantage he could get. If worse came to worst, he'd just tell her he was paranoid.

She'd managed to get the fire going by herself. She'd pulled the sofa up close, and she lay curled up, a lap rug pulled around her. The chill was already seeping into the air— even with the fire he doubted that throw would be enough. And he didn't dare offer to warm her up.

The firelight sent dancing patterns across her face. She accepted the glass of sherry with murmured thanks, and pulled her feet up to make room for him on the high-backed sofa.

He sat, because if he'd refused, it would have meant admitting how much she affected him. It was a big, enveloping couch. Room for both of them. Room for them to stretch out. Side by side. Him on top of her. Beneath her. Inside her.

"You're safe, James," she murmured. "I promise I won't make another pass at you."

He leaned back, staring at her out of hooded eyes. "That would probably be a smart idea, Annie. I'm not your type. Too old, too dull."

"Are you?"

"Believe it." He stretched out his legs in front of him, aware that she'd somehow managed to move closer to him.

"What if I told you I liked my men old and dull?"

"I'd say tough shit. I'm not doing this, Annie. Not to you, not to Win."

"I don't think Win wants to go to bed with you," she said with a hint of laughter.

He didn't laugh with her, though he knew he should make the effort. "He'll be home soon, Annie," he said patiently. "And if the power hasn't come on by then, Win'll make sure it happens. No one ever denies Win anything."

He didn't expect an argument, and he didn't get one. "True enough," she said, crossing the distance between them, leaning against his shoulder. "I wish I took after him instead of my mother."

Despite her closeness he knew she'd accepted defeat. He only wished he could accept triumph. "Be glad you're not like him, Annie," he said in a rough voice.

It was more than he ever should have said to her. But some saving grace kept her from questioning him. Instead she simply sighed, pulling the lap robe firmly around her. And James leaned back and put his arm around her, pulling her closer, letting her rest against his shoulder.

And that was the way Win found them.

Chapter Eleven

Annie's hands were still trembling when she poured a cup of instant coffee. She hated instant coffee—she considered it undrinkable. But it was sometime after dawn on a bleak desert morning, and there was nothing but instant in the shabby trailer.

She could still feel his hands around her throat. His hips against hers as he'd straddled her on the bed. He'd had an erection. They'd both known it, and she'd accused him of being sexless on purpose. To see if she could goad him into proving otherwise.

It was odd, this long-buried urge to push him. To make him look at her, touch her, see her. It felt uncomfortably familiar, and she wished she could believe her own words.

But James McKinley wasn't sexless. Never had been, although for the past few years he'd done a damned good job of convincing her he was.

She could feel him watching her, and she looked up. He was lounging in the doorway of the bedroom. He pushed away from the wall, coming toward her, and she felt a sudden panic. It was what she wanted, and yet it terrified her. There was too much riding on this, and once he touched her there'd be no turning back.

He reached her. He took her coffee mug from her and set it down on the cracked formica counter. And then he came closer, backing her up against the cabinets, entrapping her there, with his arms on either side of her, imprisoning her.

She held very still, waiting. Waiting for him. He was moving closer, dipping his head down, blocking out the murky light, when the sound of a car broke the dawn stillness.

He froze, and for a moment she knew she'd been dismissed, forgotten, as he concentrated on the sound of that automobile that drove straight up to their ramshackle trailer.

The engine was silenced. One door opened and then slammed shut; one pair of footsteps came up the rickety stairs. One fist pounded on the door.

She opened her mouth to say something, but as quick as a snake he moved, twisting her around and covering her mouth with his hand. She could feel the gun in his other hand, and the cold metal against her waist shocked her. She struggled for a brief moment, but he subdued her quickly, painfully, and she subsided, leaning back against him, gasping for breath.

"You there, McKinley?" Martin Paulsen's voice came from the other side of the metal door. "Carew sent me after you to blow your brains out and get rid of Annie as well. You gonna leave me out here like a sitting duck, or are you going to let me in and let me have a closer shot at the two of you?"

The tension drained from James's rigid body, and he set her away from him. "Are you alone?" he called out, pitching his voice low enough that it could be heard on the other side of the metal door and no farther.

"Give me a break, James. I wouldn't bring those bastards with me and you know it."

"You might not have had any choice in the matter. Carew can be pretty persuasive."

Martin's sigh of disgust was completely audible. "Listen, James, you may be the best in the business, but that doesn't mean the rest of us are slackers. I can get where I need to go without being followed. Now, are you going to let me in, or am I going to continue to freeze my ass in this desert?"

James was already unfastening the door. For the first time Annie noticed the steel bar he'd set across it in addition to the array of locks.

It would have taken her five minutes to unfasten all the hardware that locked them in there. James disposed of it in less than thirty seconds.

She'd seen her ex-husband just before she left on this insane journey of discovery. He'd been the one to tell her where to find McKinley, and now she didn't know whether it was a curse or a blessing.

He looked so very normal, jarringly so as he closed and locked the door behind him just as efficiently as James had unlocked it. And then he held up his arms, presenting himself to his old friend. "Want to check for weapons?"

Annie closed her eyes for a moment as a wave of nausea washed over her. She was Alice through the looking glass—everything was strange, topsy-turvy. Martin looked the same to her, from his handsome, slightly craggy face to his trim, muscular body dressed in Eddie Bauer's best. And he stood perfectly still as his best friend checked him for weapons, as if this were all part of his normal experience. And she realized with a shock that it was.

If Win and James weren't what she'd always assumed them to be, neither was Martin. The man she'd been married to, the man she'd shared everything with, had lived a lie.

He glanced over at her, and his smile was

rueful. "Looks like you're not in Kansas any-more, Annie," he said lightly.

James stepped back, clearly satisfied that one of the few people he supposedly trusted wasn't going to kill him. "She's known that for a while. Why'd you send her to me, Martin?"

"I figured it was time she knew the truth."

"But I don't," she said sharply.

"I don't know if anyone does," Martin said. "You got any more of that coffee, Annie?"

"It's instant."

"I'm not fussy."

The Martin she knew, the Martin she'd spent three years of married life with, insisted on Sumatran beans, dark-roasted and freshly ground. Annie shrugged, turning away from him to deal with the coffee, deceptively docile.

James threw himself down on the ratty sofa, seemingly at ease. "How'd you find out where we'd gone, Martin?" he asked gently.

"Give me a break, Mack. I can find out what I need to know. The fact of the matter is, Clancy trusted me, even if you didn't feel like you could." Martin didn't seem the slightest bit offended by that fact. "He thought you might need someone else to cover your back. In case something happened to him. And he was right about that, wasn't he?"

James's expression didn't change. "Why are you here, Martin?"

"To help you."

"What if I said we don't need any help?" he said.

"Don't be an asshole. You need all the help you can get. You may be close to invulnerable, but sooner or later someone's gonna catch up with you. I don't want Annie around when that happens."

"So you've appointed yourself my body-guard?"

"Don't be so damned amused. I'm good, and you know it."

"Not as good as I am."

"You want me to get a tape measure to see which one is bigger?" Annie demanded from the kitchen.

Martin's laugh was easy, familiar. "James always wins," he said. He took the rickety, straight-back chair, turned it around, and straddled it. His voice dropped. "I'm sorry about Clancy."

"Yeah," said James. "It happens."

"So what's the plan?"

"That depends. You still haven't told me how you managed to get here without Carew knowing. Where does he think you are? And how did you get out of the little clean-up detail?"

"You mean L.A.? I flat-out refused. Told

him I couldn't do a decent job—I was too conflicted. Carew probably knew the truth."

"And what's that?"

"I was scared shitless. I'm no match for you, James, and we both know it."

He didn't even blink. "Did Carew send Mary Margaret after me?"

Martin looked startled. "I don't know. She doesn't even work for him anymore. Since Win's death she's kept a low profile."

Annie brought Martin his coffee. There was no other place to sit but the sagging loveseat next to James. She didn't want to. But she was even more loath to show it bothered her.

"I haven't seen Mary Margaret in years," she said as she perched gingerly next to James, careful not to brush up against him. She could feel Martin's eyes on her, watching the physical byplay, and she knew him well enough to know he would jump to conclusions. She wondered whether they'd be the right ones. "What's she been doing with herself?"

"She's dead."

She turned to James, and something in his flat tone goaded her. "Does everyone around you die, James?"

He flinched. That very human reaction surprised her, but a moment later it was gone. "Sooner or later, Annie," he said. "You got any more of that coffee?"

"Get it yourself."

His mouth curved in a smile that was far from pleasant as he glanced over at Martin. "As you can see, we haven't exactly hit it off. It's just as well you're here—maybe you'll keep me from murdering her."

A look flashed between the two, so brief she didn't have time to decipher it. And then Martin smiled up at her with his old charm. For some reason it left her unmoved.

"What James is trying to say is that we need to talk without you listening, Annie. Why don't you go into the kitchen and make a lot of noise? Cook us some breakfast or something while James and I confer?"

She didn't move. "You can't pat me on the head and dismiss me the way my father used to, Martin. Too much has happened in the past six months. The past few days."

Martin froze, staring at her as if she'd suddenly grown another head. "I'm afraid Annie isn't the docile, unquestioning creature you remember," James said with a lazy drawl. "If we want to get rid of her, we'll either need to threaten her, knock her out, or tie her up."

"You haven't tied me up yet," she snapped.

"There's always a first time," he replied evenly.

"I'm not really into this tiresome macho

posturing," she said. "How about I go for a walk?"

"Sorry," James said, sounding not the least bit sorry. "I don't know if it's safe yet. Go into the kitchen and turn on the radio."

It was an order, not to be disobeyed. For a brief moment Annie considered doing just that. And then cold, harsh reality settled over her. This wasn't a game they were playing. It wasn't really macho posturing. It was life and death. He'd saved her life once already. In return he expected obedience.

She was tired of being an obedient little girl. Of doing and being what other people expected of her. She was turning into her own person, and that person didn't slink away politely when she was dismissed.

"Or I'll tie you to the bed," James added sweetly.

"Don't overplay your hand, James," she muttered gracelessly. "You're just lucky I'm hungry."

She wasn't, of course. The crackly AM radio could pick up only salsa music, but she turned it up anyway. CNN was a reasonable alternative, but she didn't want to risk hearing about the California brush fires, or the bodies found in that tiny rose-covered cottage.

She stood at the stained, rusty sink and peered out the obscured window, ignoring the quiet murmur of voices in the sitting area. The sun had come up, and the bright light of the desert day fought past the greasy coating of the window. She could see a couple of trailers in the distance, in equally bad shape, and a few abandoned cars. And the barren landscape, going on for miles upon endless miles.

Where the hell were they? And did she really want to know? Where were they going? Were they going to find the answers she needed?

She leaned forward, resting on her forearms. There was a cockroach crawling in the sink, a small one, and she considered squashing it. She couldn't bring herself to do it. There'd been too much death in the past few days. Let James the hunter do it.

She thought about revenge. She'd toyed with the notion for months now, as her belief in her father's murder grew. Someone had killed him, the man who'd been the center of her life, her guiding force, her mentor. Someone had ruthlessly snuffed out his life in his prime, and she desperately needed to know who had done it, and why.

She didn't necessarily need revenge. She could count on McKinley for that. Once he found the man who murdered Winston Sutherland, he'd destroy him. And Annie could finally put the past to rest.

But she needed answers. And she wouldn't rest until she got them.

"How much does she know?" Martin pitched his voice low enough so that there was no way Annie could overhear.

"Enough. Too damned much."

"Does she know what happened to her father?"

"She knows he was terminated."

"Does she know why?"

Their eyes met. It had never been discussed, yet James had little doubt that Martin knew as much as anyone about Win's death. If James had been Win's oldest protégé, Martin had been his dearest.

There'd been a time when James had been jealous of Martin. Martin had been and done what Win wanted. He'd been groomed to take Win's place, to take Win's daughter, when it became clear that James would never lose himself completely to Win's causes.

But in the end he had lost himself. He was nothing but a soulless shell. And Martin had survived.

"No," James said after a moment. "She doesn't know."

"Are you going to tell her?"

"You think I'm crazy? Why the hell would I tell her?"

"Because you have a perverse sense of honor. I know you, James. They may call you Dr. Death, but deep inside you're still human. You probably need confession and absolution."

"I haven't been a Catholic in thirty years."

"And Annie's not the Holy Mother. That doesn't mean you won't do something stupid and self-sacrificing."

"It would mean her death."

"Yeah, well, you could probably find some justification in that. You iced Mary Margaret, didn't you? Have you slept with Annie yet?"

He'd almost forgotten how cool and clinical Martin could be. It was one of the things he despised most about him. It was one of the things he most needed from him.

"No."

"Why not? You know perfectly well the best way to bind someone to you is to fuck her. Make her emotionally and physically dependent on you. You aren't the type to let sentiment get in your way—you do what needs to be done. Why haven't you slept with her?"

James glanced over at her. She was standing at the sink, staring out through the grimy window, her back straight and strong, her hair tangled from sleep. He wasn't about to explain to Martin that he wanted her too much.

"Maybe I was saving her for you," he said

lazily. "I thought you'd probably show up sooner or later. You usually do."

"Just like a bad penny. Hey, I'm not picky. I don't mind your leftovers, if you don't mind mine. She's not into Mary Margaret's kinky games, but she's actually quite . . . endearing in bed. I'd take her back in a flash if she wanted it."

Endearing. The phrase was damnably evocative. James forced himself to smile. "Maybe you should take care of it, then. She's used to you—it would make things easier."

Martin shook his head. "Not that I wouldn't mind. She's the one who broke off our relationship, not me. But I don't scare her the way you do. You've always had a powerful effect on people when you choose to exert it. If you want her too overwhelmed to question orders, you're gonna have to be the one to do her." He laughed, half to himself. "Would you listen to us? It sounds like we're talking about some unpleasant chore. Trust me, I wish I could justify taking over. But in this case, keeping the two of you alive is the first priority, and you stand a better chance of that if you're the one."

"I think I can handle it," James said in a cool voice.

"You just need to handle her right," Martin continued, ignoring the warning signals.

"She's amazingly timid about sex. Got all these hang-ups, neuroses. You gotta do her in the dark with her nightgown on, so help me, God. Otherwise she freezes up, and nothing can loosen her. I blame Win for it. I think he must have had some Wagnerian governess brainwash her."

"Are you finished settling the fate of the world yet?" Annie had turned from the sink, calling out over the sound of the radio.

"We're getting there," Martin said cheerfully. "Make us some breakfast, would you?"

The look she cast Martin was laced with pure irritation, a fact which pleased James. But that pleasure worried him. He didn't like the fact that Annie had slept with Martin again. Didn't like the image of the two of them, in the dark, under the covers. Didn't like it so much that he was having a hard time trusting the only man in the department he could count on.

"Listen, I'll make myself scarce and you take care of it. Whaddya need—a couple of hours? More? Less?"

James looked at his hand. It wasn't curled into a fist—it was resting loosely on his thigh. It was amazing how instinct always kicked in. "It depends," he murmured. "Why are you in such a goddamned hurry? Do you want to watch?"

Martin grinned. "Not through your windows, buddy. She's like a time bomb waiting to go off, and there's only one way to defuse her. If you don't do it, I will."

"Be my guest."

"Nope. It's you she wants, in case you haven't figured that out yet. And I want what's best for you. She makes you vulnerable. If you're vulnerable, then the whole damned house of cards may collapse. As soon as you get this taken care of, then you'll be more in control."

"You think I'm not in control?" he murmured in a lazy voice.

"You're always in control, man. But this is the biggest mess we've ever been in. I just think we should cover all our bases."

"That's one way to put it. I could always kill her."

"Yeah," Martin agreed calmly. "And it might come to that. But you don't really want to, do you?"

"Maybe that's exactly why I should do it."

Martin shook his head. "She knows stuff, James. I'm willing to bet you. Stuff she doesn't know she knows. You silence her now and we'll never find out. And if we don't, we're dead men."

"We already are."

"Speak for yourself. I have a lot of plans for my future."

James looked at his old friend. Martin was almost ten years younger, the product of the kind of Ivy League background Win had concocted for James. Princeton, Yale Law School, a good family. Perhaps it was just as much of a lie as James's past. It didn't matter. What mattered was the knowledge, the bond between them.

"You know, you'd make a hell of a pimp," James said dryly. "You missed your calling."

"Not necessarily," Martin said. He rose, and James watched him, instinctively prepared for any sudden moves. Martin wouldn't make them, but old habits died hard. James wouldn't have trusted his mother if she were still alive. "I'll make myself scarce. You know what you're going to do next?"

"I have an idea. Win was in Northern Ireland right before he died. It seems as good a place as any to start looking. He must have had a reason for being there."

Martin's grin was faint. "What do you think about that? How long has it been?"

"I don't have any problems with it," he said evenly. "I've been back any number of times."

"On clear-cut jobs. This is different. You know that. And you'll have Annie with you."

"You think I can't handle it, Martin?" he said in his softest voice.

Martin looked momentarily unnerved, which pleased James. "You can handle just about anything. I'll be back later."

Annie had switched off the radio, eyeing the two of them suspiciously. "Have you finished your little conspiracy?" she demanded.

Before Win died she wouldn't have demanded a thing. Even Martin looked startled at her tone of voice, and he cast an amused, commiserating glance at James.

"All finished, Annie," Martin said smoothly. "I'll be back in a few hours. I've got some things to do."

"Can I go with you? I feel claustrophobic."

"No." James's voice was cool and implacable. He waited for her protest, but she said nothing, merely glaring at him as Martin let himself out of the trailer.

She followed him to the door, and James half expected her to try to dart out after him. He tensed, ready to leap and stop her, but she simply closed the door behind him and began fastening the locks. She was clumsy but determined, and he watched her out of hooded eyes, fascinated.

It took her almost five minutes. When she was finished, she turned and faced him, and there was no missing the faint look of triumph in her eyes. "I figured I'd better know how to do that for myself. I don't like being dependent."

"No?" he said softly.

"I spent twenty-seven years that way. It was enough."

"I don't know if right now is the time to start developing a life of your own," he murmured.

"Too late."

"Too late," he echoed, watching her.

"What were you and Martin talking about? Why did he suddenly disappear?" She was just out of reach, but he knew he could move quickly. He watched her, idly, and wondered how he ought to take her. Fast, so she couldn't object. So she didn't even know what hit her?

Or a slow seduction that left her a weak-limbed puddle in the bed.

Though right now he couldn't begin to imagine Annie Sutherland as weak.

"So did you two decide what we're going to do next?" she asked.

"In a manner of speaking. We were discussing who was going to take you to bed."

"Sure you were, James," she scoffed. "Who lost? You?"

"I'm here, aren't I?"

"Exactly." She turned away from him, heading into the kitchen. "I hope Martin's gone food shopping. There's nothing to eat but re-fried beans, and I'm really not in the mood, no matter how much salsa music is on the radio. I want—"

She hadn't heard him come up behind her. He could move very swiftly, silently when he wanted to, and this time he wanted to. He put his arms around her, his hands on her breasts, and pulled her against him, tight.

It shut her up immediately. She stood very still, and he could feel the faint tremor that washed over her body. She wasn't nearly as tough as she wanted to be. As she wanted him to believe.

He cupped her breasts, running his thumbs over her nipples. They hardened, as his cock hardened against her, and he told himself Martin was right. The sooner he did it, the sooner he'd stop thinking about it. He couldn't afford to waste even a fraction of his attention on the softness of Annie Sutherland's skin, the warmth of her breath, the sweet, musky scent of her that was driving him crazy.

He slid one hand down her stomach, over the loose-fitting running shorts and between her legs, pressing up against her, imagining the heat and dampness, the need. She made a strangled cry of protest, but then no other sound. She simply let him hold her tightly against him as his hand rode between her legs.

Martin was right, he thought absently. She was shivering now, so damned ready to explode he almost came thinking about it. He thought about shoving her shorts down, bending her over the kitchen counter and taking her from the back. Without having to look at her face, without having to kiss her. Without having to acknowledge this was anything but a straight fuck, something they both needed.

He shoved his hand down inside her loose pants. She wasn't wearing any underwear, and she was wet. He knew she would be.

She fought him for a moment, but he ignored her struggles. He was much, much stronger than she was, and he wasn't interested in her protests, in denial or shyness or whatever. He slid his fingers deep into her, using his thumb, and he made her come.

The sound she made was low, desperate, and lost. She was a fierce knot of reaction in his grasp, and he held her, prolonging it, touching her, pushing at her, feeling the wave after wave of response that hit her.

"Stop," she gasped, but he wouldn't stop. She was shaking apart, and he wouldn't let her go, let her rest. He wasn't sure what he wanted from her. He needed something beyond complete surrender, beyond the powerful climaxes he was wringing from her. He wanted to drain the fight, the life from her. He wanted her soul.

He took it. Sliding his fingers deep inside her, listening to her choking cry, he took everything from her.

She was weeping. He knew that as he felt her tormented body collapse in his arms. He was supporting her—her legs had no strength, and all she could do was sob quietly.

He released her. Pulled his hand from her shorts, set her against the counter, and stepped back. For a moment he reached for his zipper and then stopped.

She had her face on the counter. The sobs were softer now but no less shattering. And he realized it might be kinder if he simply leaned over, kissed her behind her ear, and killed her. Kinder for both of them.

He turned and left the kitchen area of the tiny trailer. Left her alone, broken, weeping. He flicked on the television to CNN and threw himself back onto the sagging love seat. And only when he turned up the sound did he allow himself to breathe.

He had no idea how long she'd lie there and cry. How long he could stand to listen to it. He'd heard many women cry over the years. Women mourning their children, cut down by sniper fire. Women whining that he didn't love them. Women dying, and afraid.

He didn't let women's tears bother him.

But Annie's did. And he hoped to God she'd stop.

It wasn't until a momentary lull on the television that he noticed the silence. He looked up, and she was standing in the kitchen, staring at him, her face pale, shocky, tear-streaked. He hadn't kissed her, he thought, with a mixture of despair and relief. He hadn't made the mistake of kissing her.

And then he noticed the gun she was holding.

Chapter Twelve

"Are you going to shoot me, Annie? Isn't that a little extreme?"

She knew how to fire a gun. Her father had despised guns, but he'd made certain his daughter knew how to use one, and James's gun was not dissimilar from the 9mm weapon she had practiced on. He could move fast, she'd seen him to do it, but not faster than a bullet.

"No," she said, setting the gun down on the countertop with great care, close enough that she could pick it up quickly. "As long as you don't touch me again."

His gaze was steady, unreadable, but he made no effort to move, to take the gun out of her reach. "Then you'd better shoot me, Annie," he said, turning his gaze back to the television.

She wanted to. She wanted to pick up the gun and wipe that cool, enigmatic expression from his face. Just once she wanted to see whether he could feel anything.

During the long days after her father's death he'd been there, a solid, secure presence, looking after the details she'd been too distraught to deal with, an invisible strength for her to turn to. But not once during all that time, even when they lowered Win's walnut and brass coffin into the ground at Arlington, did he betray any emotion.

She shivered, remembering that cold spring day. A bitter rain had been falling, a fitting cap to the week, and James had stood beside her in a dark raincoat, holding a black umbrella over her head. She'd watched the coffin being lowered with a sense of numb horror that had haunted her dreams ever since.

"I want to be cremated."

That got his attention. He stared at her, then leaned over and killed the sound on the TV. "You aren't going to die," he said.

"Everyone's going to die sooner or later. The way things have been going lately, I suspect it's going to be sooner."

"I'm not going to let anyone kill you."

"Martin said you're good, but you're not perfect." Her knees were still weak from what he'd done to her in the kitchen. She was wet between her legs, angry and vulnerable. She moved from behind the counter, away from the gun, wondering if she'd regret it.

"What made you think of that?" He leaned back, looking at her.

"I hated Win's funeral."

"It wasn't supposed to be fun."

"He insisted on a full burial. I hated it. When I die, I want to be burned and my ashes put in a tiny little box. You can keep me on your mantel."

She'd managed to shake him. Something crossed his face, something oddly akin to horror, swiftly followed by anger.

"Fine," he snapped. "Though I might prefer to keep you in some Tupperware."

"No plastic," she said, pushing him. He didn't strike her as a man capable of feeling horror. But she hadn't mistaken his reaction. "I'll settle for an empty tequila bottle. One without the worm. I imagine you'll have no trouble finding one of those."

"You can be a real bitch, you know that, Annie?" he said calmly enough.

The notion startled her. "No," she said, more to herself than to him. "I hadn't known that." She wanted to get away from him, but there was nowhere in the enclosed space where she could escape. The one place she didn't intend to go was the bed. She sat down in the cracked vinyl chair. "I don't think Win would recognize me nowadays."

"You'd probably piss the hell out of him."

"Why?" She was shocked.

"Because he did his damnedest to make you who he wanted you to be. Intelligent, well behaved, conservatively dressed. A model daughter and the perfect wife for whoever he chose for you."

"Not such a perfect wife, and he didn't choose Martin," she snapped. "And what's wrong with that description?"

"It's not you. It's who he made you. And you let him do it. You let him drain all the life and individuality from you, until you didn't have a thought or an emotion to call your own. The model young Republican with just enough liberal notions to make you politically correct."

"At least I have emotions."

"They weren't yours."

"They are now. Including a really intense hatred of you, James," she said in an icy voice.

He smiled. Slow, disbelieving, and so infuriating that she wished the gun was still in reach. "Annie," he said softly, "if you want to believe that you go right ahead."

She glared at him. "Are you egocentric enough to assume I still have a crush on you? I got over that years ago, James. All I want from you is the name of my father's killer. And the reason."

"That's all? You don't want revenge?"

"I assumed you'd take care of that part," she said stiffly.

"Oh, did you? We find out who executed your father, and then you get to leave the dirty work up to me. You can go back to your safe little life and your drab clothes with clean hands and a satisfied conscience. Is that it?"

"I'd really like to kill you," she said.

"I seem to bring out your violent streak, don't I?" he murmured. "Maybe we'd better bring our unholy alliance to an end before you turn out just like me."

"And what would that be like? Or don't you even know?" she goaded him.

"I know," he said, and his voice was bleak. "When Martin comes back, I'll send you with him. He may not be as good as I am, but he has connections. He could keep Carew off your back. If anyone can keep you safe, Martin can."

"Can anyone keep me safe?"

She expected a lie, an evasion. "I don't know," he said.

"Then I'm not going with him."

He was showing emotion now. Anger. He pushed off the couch, stalked by her, and it took all her courage not to pull her legs away from him as he brushed by. "You'll goddamned well do as I say."

"Make me."

He stopped, mid-stride, turning to look at her, and she regretted her words instantly. "Haven't I just given you a clear lesson on how I can make you do anything I want you to do? I can overpower you, physically, sexually, emotionally. You'll do what I tell you."

"I'll fight back."

His exasperated sigh was a little warning, and then he leaned over her, trapping her in the chair, his hands on the vinyl arms, his face close to hers. "You won't win, Annie," he said softly. "No one ever wins."

Anne stared up at him. His face was so close she could see the specks of silver in his dark eyes, the bleakness he tried to disguise. She didn't want to think about what he'd just done to her, or why.

"I don't want a battle, James," she said. "And neither do you. Just help me find out what happened to my father."

"It's not that simple."

"I'll make it simple," she cried. "Find out what happened to that picture of the saint. Find out what he did with it, and we'll stop there. If you want to."

"If I want to," he echoed. The trailer was absolutely silent, only the faint, muffled sound of the muted TV disturbing the thick tension that lay between them. "All right," he said. "We'll find what he did with the picture. And then you'll go back to Martin."

She didn't want to go back to Martin, she realized with sudden shock. She never did again.

But she refused to consider what she really did want. "Find the picture," she said, "and I'll do what you tell me to."

He stared at her for a minute longer, then nodded, moving into the kitchen, busying himself with the kettle.

She glanced at the television. The mute was on, but the pictures were bright and vivid. It looked like a bombed nightclub, somewhere in Europe. Covered bodies were stretched out over a wide floor, and there were dark-clothed women weeping in silent fury.

She shuddered, looking away. Death was everywhere. In the past six months, since she'd first discovered her father's body at the bottom of the stairs, she'd been living with mortality. She'd always been afraid of death—avoiding funerals and tragic movies and even the obligatory sympathy notes. Now she'd been flung into the heart of it, and there was no longer any room for fear.

"Don't send me away, James," she said quietly.

He didn't turn, and for a moment she thought he hadn't heard her. But he had. "It would be better if you left it up to me," he said finally. "I'll take care of things. I'm good at cleaning up the mess people make."

"I don't want you to. I don't want someone's death on your soul, no matter how well deserved. I just want to find out what really happened to Win. And then we can leave it at that."

He turned, and she stared at him, mesmerized. Even though it was mid-morning, the trailer was dark, the dim lightbulbs barely penetrating the gloom. "Annie, I lost my soul years ago."

He believed it. And it was then that she realized she was still half in love with him, just as she'd been when she was younger and he'd been strong and mysterious and there.

He believed he'd lost his soul, and he was trying to convince her as well. But in this case she knew him better than he knew himself. He wouldn't be hurting if he were soulless. And he was hurting so badly.

She wanted to get up and put her arms around him. She wanted to draw his head down to her breast and nurture him. Murmur soft, soothing words to comfort him, heal him. She wanted to take him into that rumpled bed, into her arms, into her body, and show him . . .

"Stop looking at me like that!"

It snapped her out of her erotic reverie like a glass of ice water thrown in her face. "Like what?"

"Like I'm a wounded sparrow and you're Saint Francis."

He managed to startle a laugh out of her. "Actually, my thoughts were a bit more secular."

Fortunately, he didn't follow up on that. "You can't save me, Annie. You can't save anyone but yourself."

"Who says I want to save you?"

"The look in your eye. That all-he-needs-is-a-good-woman-to-love-him look. You're old enough and smart enough to know better."

"I hadn't noticed I was volunteering," she shot back.

He shook his head. "You're a bleeding heart, Annie. Win couldn't wipe that out of you. You think you can make things better. But you can't. Some things are beyond mending, and all you can do is wipe up the blood and get on with it."

"Life isn't that grim," she protested.

"The hell it's not!" She'd wanted emotion, and now she got it, in an explosion of fury. "Life's a dirty, bloody, hopeless business for most people, and there's nothing you can do to change it. You can just go back to your safe world and pretend it didn't happen. Mourn your father and let go. Get married again, to Martin or whoever, and have babies if you want. You can make love in the dark, and no one will try to scare you. But keep out of this mess."

"What mess?"

"My life."

She considered it for a moment, and then a thought struck her, an icy, chilling one. "What did you mean about making love in the dark?" she asked calmly.

"I know everything about you. You have no secrets, didn't you realize that? Win could find out everything, and he passed it along. I know you got your period when you were fourteen, and you were worried because it was so late. I know you've slept with five men in your life, including Martin. I know you don't like oral sex or doing it with the lights on or anything other than missionary position with your eyes closed. You worried you were frigid, your shoe size is eight and a half A, and you had a crush on me from the time you were nineteen years old until you were twenty-one. Do you want to hear more?"

"My therapist's records," she said numbly.

"No one could keep anything from Win."

"But why did he tell you?" She couldn't keep the weary defeat from her voice. She felt betrayed, by her father, by the man in front of her who seemed so angry.

"He wanted to torment me."

Her head jerked up. She stared at him in disbelieving shock, but before she could say anything there was a sudden pounding on the door.

It startled the hell out of her. It didn't ruffle him in the slightest, and she realized he must have known someone was out there all along. And he'd deliberately made such a provocative statement, knowing she couldn't demand any kind of explanation.

"It's me," Martin called from the other side of the door.

James was already unfastening the locks. "I know," he said, his back to Annie. Martin slipped inside, bearing bags of groceries and a ready smile on his face.

"Food," he announced cheerfully, dumping the bags on the kitchen counter and pulling out chips and beer, frozen dinners and Diet Coke. His eyes narrowed as he took in Annie's expression. "So what have you two been doing while I was gone?"

"Go to hell," James snapped. "She's yours. Take her with you when you leave." And a moment later he was out of the trailer, slamming the heavy metal door behind him.

The silence was absolute. And then Martin opened a can of soda and handed it to Annie. "I take it you two aren't getting along?"

"You could say so," she replied.

Martin shrugged. "I suppose I should say I'm sorry, but I'm not. I was a fool to have sent you after him, Annie. It was a major mistake on my part, but I didn't realize . . ."

"Didn't realize what?" she prodded when he didn't finish his sentence.

Martin shook his head, then peered at her from under the shaggy brown strands. "What do you know about what he and Win did? What has he told you?"

Annie shrugged. "It sounded like they were playing junior G-men, or James Bond or something. A lot of macho spy games from out of the Cold War paranoia. James said you were part of it as well."

Martin leaned across the counter, and his eyes were dark and troubled. "I suppose that's true enough. Win was the head of a covert organization dealing with security matters."

"Spying," Annie said flatly.

"If you want to call it that," Martin agreed. "Just the covert gathering of information. It didn't do anyone any harm, except our so-called enemies, and it provided a useful balance of power. That's where I worked. Not actually gathering the information, but sorting it, disseminating it, covering things up."

"It sounds childish enough," Annie said.

"It was anything but. There was a branch to Win's little organization. I hate to admit that he knew about it, but I think it's time you realized that your father wasn't the sweet, absentminded old gentleman you thought he was."

"I know that, Martin," she said calmly.

"He was a brilliant, ruthless manipulator. He'd use anybody or anything to accomplish what he thought was right."

She didn't want to hear this, she thought distantly. She wanted to follow James out into the desert sunshine, her hands over her ears, running.

But there was no way she could stop him from telling her, no way she could escape. She'd hidden from reality for far too long in her life. Martin was right—it was time to face the truth.

"Tell me," she said in a husky voice.

"Win set up a covert branch of his department. None of us knew about it—certainly not Carew, or me, or any of the others. We weren't supposed to. It was just Win and his favorite son and one or two others. James was his creature—he did what he was told."

"And what did Win tell him to do?"

"Kill."

She wanted to throw up. She'd known death had followed them wherever they'd gone, the deadly stink of the blood lily haunting her dreams. But the flat reality, from a man she trusted, was stomach-churning.

"Who?"

"It all started out nobly enough. Anyone who seemed a danger to Win's idea of a proper world order. Dictators. Terrorist leaders. Politicians. People who would interfere in the United States' best interests abroad. Win would make the decision, give the orders, and James or one of the others would carry them out."

"The others?"

"Mary Margaret Hanover. Clancy. I'm not sure how many more," Martin said.

"And you didn't know anything about it? You worked with both of them for the last ten years?" she cried in disbelief.

"I'm not a fool, Annie. I suspected something wasn't right. Too many coincidences. Too many convenient disappearances. Let me make one thing clear—I agreed with Win that most of these people were a very real danger to world peace. I even, for my sins, helped single them out. But I didn't agree with how he handled it. How he had James handle it."

"But why would he do it? Why would he agree?" Annie demanded, bewildered.

"Patriotism. James is very old-fashioned—he won't admit it, but his country comes first to him. And he'd do anything Win would tell him. Most of us would, you included."

Annie shivered. "What do you think happened?"

"Things started getting a little out of hand. Some of the hits turned out to be of dubious political value. Money started changing hands. Things got corrupted," he said carefully.

"Things?"

"Jesus, Annie, I don't want to tell you this," he said desperately. She stared at him, implacable, waiting. "All right, your father got corrupted. He started hiring out his talented little squad of handpicked assassins to the highest bidder. Carew or someone above him discovered exactly what he was doing. Someone was dispatched to take your father out of the equation, quietly, without a lot of fuss. And they've been after James ever since. He didn't go off to the Caribbean to drown his sorrows. He was running for his life."

"And you sent me down to him."

"I told you, I didn't realize the truth. I still don't know half of it. If you still want to find out what happened, James is the man who knows the answers. If he doesn't, he knows how to get them, and he's not squeamish about how he does it. But he's right, we need to get you safely away from here. Leave it up to him, Annie."

"No."

Martin stared at her in patent disbelief. "What do you mean, no? Haven't you listened to a word I said? James is a man who kills for a living. Do you realize how many people he's killed in the time you've been with him?"

"I don't want to know."

"Three in Mexico. Including Mary Margaret Hanover. You remember her, don't you? One of your father's protégés?"

"I remember her," she said numbly.

"Four more in California. Including his old friend Clancy."

"He didn't kill Clancy!" Annie cried.

"Who else could have? You have to face the truth. James is like an animal. A killing machine. He'll get the job done and not count the cost. You can't make a house pet out of him, Annie."

"He trusts you, Martin."

Martin shook his head. "James doesn't trust anyone, me included. For what it's worth, I think he's a brilliant, dedicated man. He'll find out what happened to your father, and he'll take care of things. Before someone finally manages to get to him. But in the meantime